CHANCE OF A LIFETIME

SUSAN HAYES

Copyright © 2020 Susan Hayes

Chance of a Lifetime

First Print Publication: April 2020

Cover Design: Mina Carter

Editor: Dayna Hart

Published by: Black Scroll Publications Ltd.

ISBN: 978-1-988446-61-5

DEDICATION

*For my Mum and Dad, for all their love and support.
This one also is dedicated to my readers and my fellow friends
and authors. I couldn't do this without you.*

No risk. No reward.

Erik O'Neill has finally stopped looking for trouble. Now, trouble's come looking for him. After years of cage fighting, Erik is ready to step away from the Nova Club's fight ring and into a new role – security for the club he calls home. All his plans change when a lovely loner starts visiting the club, and he finds himself caught between the need to safeguard his home and his friends, and his desire to protect the woman laying claim to his heart.

Chance is a cyborg with a secret. If the wrong people find her, she'll lose her shot at having the life she dreams of – or any life at all. She's come to the Drift looking for allies, but when she meets Erik, she discovers he can offer her more than safety. He's her chance at happiness, too.

When time runs out, she'll have to make a choice that will change her life forever - keep running, or turn to the one man her heart tells her she can trust.

PROLOGUE

Out on the edge of civilized space is a rag-tag collection of space stations and platforms known as the Drift. It's a haven for the hunted, the lost, and those seeking second chances. The people who live there hail from every species, class, and corner of the galaxy, but they all have one thing in common: they don't belong anywhere else.

There's nothing beyond the Drift but wild space and an asteroid belt full of ore-rich rocks. The asteroids are mined by hundreds of vessels and their hard-working crews. When the ships deliver their haul to be processed, those crews hit the infamous bars, casinos, and pleasure houses that are the Drift's primary source of income…and only source of entertainment.

It's a world of its own. One where corporations rule, the laws are flexible, and everything is for sale, for the right price.

WELCOME TO THE DRIFT.

CHAPTER ONE

ERIK CAUGHT sight of a tall figure navigating the crowded club and smiled. She was back. His mystery woman didn't make an appearance every night, but when she did, his life got a little extra kick.

The Nova was one of the hottest clubs on the Drift, attracting a bevy of lovely females from every species and echelon of society, but there was something about *her* that was different. For one thing, she was always alone, though he'd seen more than a few guys try to change that. She'd politely but firmly rejected each and every one of them. On two occasions, the guys hadn't got the hint, and he'd cheerfully kicked their asses out of the club and away from *his* mystery woman. Which was probably a bit presumptive of him considering he didn't even know her name. Work always got in the way.

What he did know could be summarized on the

back of a cocktail napkin. She had legs that went for light-years, a mane of chestnut waves he wanted to wrap around his fists, and a lush mouth just made for kissing. She'd been the star of every fantasy he'd had since the first night she'd walked into the club, and he wasn't letting her leave again until he knew her name.

He scanned the rest of the club, looking for trouble. It was a full house tonight, with most of the guests gathering near the fighting pit. The cage was still dark, but in less than an hour, the fights would start and the money and blood would start to flow. Most nights, it was more money than blood. The Nova only hired the best fighters, men and women who knew how to put on a good show without doing any serious damage.

He absently ran a finger along the side of his nose. The last time he'd been in the ring, his buddy, Dai, had broken it. That had been two months ago. He needed to get back in there soon and show them all he hadn't gone soft.

He looked over to the gaming area again. She was still there, the bright red streaks in her dark hair making her easy to spot. So did her height. She was only slightly shorter than he was, just a few inches shy of six feet or so, and she was the walking definition of the word statuesque.

"Have you asked her out yet, or are you hoping to initiate this romance telepathically?" Cynder appeared beside him without warning.

"*Fraxx*, Cyn! When are you going to stop doing that to me?"

"When it stops being fun." Cyn was a cyborg and her unique combination of genetic and technological enhancements had gifted her with a damned annoying level of stealth. She inclined her head toward his mystery woman. "And you didn't answer my question."

"She only shows up when I'm on duty. If I quit doing the rounds to chat her up, your brothers would kick my ass."

Cyn snorted. "No, they wouldn't. They chased Zura around this bar, on duty and off. Besides, it's obvious she's coming to see you."

"What? How is it obvious?"

The cyborg rolled her eyes. "You said it yourself. She only comes around on the days you're working. You think that's a coincidence?"

He ran a hand over his hair, smoothing the blond locks back from his face as he considered her words. *Well, hell.* "Until now? Yeah."

"It's not. And you're welcome." She gave him a light shove. "Now, go make with the talky-talk. Or do you need me to help you with that, too?"

"I can chat up my own women, thank you, boss."

"And yet here you are. I'm never going to win the betting pool if you don't get your ass in gear."

Oh fraxx *no.* He cracked his knuckles. "Who's running a pool on my love life, and how soon can I get them in the cage for a little payback?"

"Our little blue momma is running the pool, which means you can forget about payback."

"Zura? She's got twins to look after, not to mention two husbands. How the hell does she have time to run a betting pool? For that matter, how does she know I'm interested in anyone?"

Cynder uttered a low, throaty chuckle. "We're family, Erik. You can't keep secrets from your family."

"It's not a secret. It's not even a thing, yet," he grumbled.

"And it won't be, unless you go talk to her."

He glanced toward the gaming area again. He'd been looking for her, but something else caught his attention.

"Trouble?" Cyn asked, shifting to a more aggressive stance.

"Kirk's letting an intoxicated guest bet on starburst." He checked the area, but none of the senior gaming staff were around. They were probably helping deal with the rush of bets being placed on tonight's fights.

Cyn tapped her temple. "I'm letting Jaeger know there's a problem on the floor. Can you handle things until he gets back?"

"On it."

A path opened up for him as he strode through the crowded club. If his size and stormy expression didn't inspire people to move, the word "Security" emblazoned on his dark blue uniform usually clued them in.

"I'm on my way," Jaeger's voice came over his earpiece.

He didn't bother responding. He entered the relatively quiet gaming area, made his way over to

Kirk, and tapped the man on the shoulder. "I need you to put the game on hold for a minute."

Kirk shot him an irritated look. "Why?"

"Because there's a problem." A handful of gamblers and onlookers watched the byplay with interest. His mystery woman was one of them, and judging by the chips in her hand, she'd been about to make a wager.

"There's no problem." Kirk turned his back on Erik and nodded to the intoxicated player. "You're up."

Erik squelched the urge to pick the brash young dealer up by the scruff of his uniform and shake him. Instead, he shouldered Kirk out of the way and slapped a hand down on the table's controls, freezing play. "Sorry, sir. Technical difficulties."

Now he was close enough, he could see the player's pupils were dilated and his skin had a distinctly yellow cast. That coloring was a side-effect of the most popular recreational pharma currently making the rounds. The man shouldn't have been allowed near a gaming table, and Kirk had to know it. House rules banned anyone whose judgment was chemically compromised from placing bets.

"But I was winning!" the player protested.

"You're welcome to come back tomorrow and try your luck then. But this game is over."

"Asshole," the player muttered.

Kirk set a hand down on the stack of chips near his station. "Why are you shutting us down?"

Because you're violating the rules and letting an intoxicated patron play because he's a heavy tipper. Jaeger was going to tear a strip off the kid as wide as the Milky

Way when he found out. Erik ignored Kirk and offered the angry player an apologetic shrug. "Sorry. My orders are to shut down the table."

The gambler grunted. "Then I'll move to the other one. C'mon, dealer man."

Erik bit back a sigh and tried to smile pleasantly for the sake of his audience, including his lovely mystery woman. He was trying to make a good impression, damn it. Why couldn't the universe give him a break? He glanced up to find her watching him —her soft lips pursed in a tiny smile, and her pale brown eyes gleamed in silent amusement.

He tried another approach. "Maybe you should take a break, sir. Have something to eat. The fights will be starting soon. You don't want to miss those."

"Fight's starting right *fraxxing* now if you don't let me finish my game!"

The player came around the gaming table, his fists raised and lips curled back in a manic snarl. Erik dropped into a fighting crouch, his mind racing. He needed to subdue this guy fast, with minimal noise and risk to the bystanders. He was still considering options when the other man bellowed in surprise and pitched forward, his ungainly charge turning into an even uglier faceplant. He hit the floor hard enough to rattle the chips on the table. That was going to leave a mark, and possibly a dent in the floor.

Erik dropped to a crouch beside the fallen man. As he did so he spotted the reason for the asshole's swan dive. Someone had tripped him. Erik swept his gaze up a shapely leg and found himself looking up at his mystery woman. Now he *really* needed to talk to her, and then buy her a drink. Her quick actions had ended what could have been a nasty confrontation.

She flashed him a quick smile and then retreated into the fast gathering crowd of onlookers.

He was tempted to leave the fool on the floor and go after her. Where the hell was everyone, anyway?

"I leave for ten minutes, and this place falls apart. Well, it's nice to know I've got job security," Jaeger drawled from somewhere behind him.

"Please, you're married to one of the owners. You're as secure as it gets." Erik stood, turned to face Jaeger. He was standing beside his batch-brother, Toro, and the two of them took up a significant amount of real estate. Dropping his voice to a near whisper, he summarized the situation for the brothers, knowing the cyborgs would be able to hear him over the thump of the music and the buzz of the crowd.

Jaeger listened, then nodded in understanding. "Thanks for dealing with this."

"No problem. I should get back to work, though." And his first job was to track down the woman, introduce himself, and say thank you.

"We got this." Jaeger looked pointedly at Kirk. "I thought I told you to stick to the blackjack tables."

"No one was interested in blackjack," Kirk said.

"So you decided to fire up the starburst table while I wasn't around." Jaeger raised a dark brow. "Come with me, Kirk. We need to have a little talk."

Erik knew what that meant. Everyone got one

chance to screw up at the Nova. Kirk had just had his. If he messed up again, he was done.

He left the gaming area as Toro lifted the still groggy gambler to his feet. Somewhere in the crowd was a tall, leggy brunette he needed to find.

Erik scanned the club and spotted her near the bar that spanned most of one wall. Good. He hadn't missed her. He smoothed back his hair, straightened his stance, and headed straight for her. Somewhere on the far side of the club, Cynder cheered loud enough to be heard over the hubbub. "Go get her, tiger!"

"She's family. You can't kill family," he reminded himself. No matter how tempting it would be to try.

SHE SHOULDN'T HAVE GOTTEN involved. She was here to gather information. She couldn't do that if she didn't keep her distance. She needed clear data, unclouded by emotion, but when she'd seen what was about to happen, she'd stepped in without thinking. She couldn't stand by and watch Erik get hurt.

It hadn't taken long to learn the names of everyone who was part of the Nova Club family. Some of them she'd known about before she even left the cyborg colony on Liberty. The cyborg rebels of the Nova Club, and their human supporters were legends on Liberty. That's why she'd come here. She needed help, and they were the only ones she might be able to trust. Stories and whispers weren't facts, though. So, she was gathering data before she made her final decision. At least, that had been the plan.

"Hello," a male voice spoke from just behind her, confirming that her plans had fallen completely out of orbit.

She hadn't heard him speak before, but she knew it was *him*. It had to be. The low, slightly rough tones, the almost undetectable hint of a Cassien system accent that not even years in space had completely erased. She turned around to face Erik O'Neill, the only man she'd ever fantasized about. "Hello."

"I wanted to say thank you for what you did back there." He tilted his head toward the gaming area. "If you hadn't done that, I would have had to take him down. That might have gotten messy."

"He'd consumed enough Golden Dream to incapacitate most of his pain receptors. It wouldn't have been a quick fight, and others might have been injured." Based on the data, she estimated there was a thirty percent chance Erik would have been hurt in the fight, with much higher odds of one or more of the bystanders being seriously injured.

"You knew he was on Dream?" Erik asked.

She shrugged. "It was obvious from his skin tone. That's why I was about to bet against him. Starburst requires a certain amount of dexterity, and his was rapidly deteriorating." She would have made some much-needed scrip from that bet. The odds had been ninety-two percent in her favor.

"You knew he was impaired and bet anyway?"

"The game would have continued whether I bet or

not." She was still working to understand the rules of conduct most species operated by. She understood the basics: don't kill, don't hurt others, don't steal. It was the more nebulous rules that gave her trouble. Should she not have placed a bet? Why not?

Erik considered that for a moment, then nodded. "True enough. My name's Erik, by the way. What's yours?"

"Chance." It was the name she'd chosen for herself. So much nicer than the string of numbers she'd been assigned at Reamus research station.

"Would you allow me to buy you a drink, Chance? As a thank you for helping out, and to take some of the sting out of your lost winnings." He smiled, and her pulse jumped to light speed. He really was exceptionally attractive when he smiled. She liked the way his eyes crinkled a bit at the corners.

"I'd like that."

His smile widened and he offered her his hand. She took it, expecting him to shake it in a standard human greeting. Instead, he raised her hand to his lips and placed a chaste kiss to the back of her hand. A tingle of pleasure rushed up her arm at the simple contact, and she had to bite back a soft gasp of surprise.

"Great. Let's find a free table."

He walked just ahead of her, checking over his shoulder several times to make sure she was still behind him. Their positions gave her a nice view of his physique. She had gathered enough information to know that despite his build, he wasn't a cyborg. His strength and power were a combination of good genetics and years of training, nothing more. But it certainly looked good on him.

They arrived at the velvet ropes that cordoned off the VIP section from the rest of the club. It wasn't full yet, but it would be soon. It had the best vantage points for watching the fights.

There was another security guard watching the entrance, but he stepped aside and let Erik pass with a friendly nod. She knew him, too. Dai Amari.

"I'm taking my break. Call me if there's trouble," Erik told him.

"Toro's working tonight. We could all take the rest of the night off and he wouldn't notice."

"He'd probably love it. Kit and Luke wouldn't. That man is hard on the furniture."

The other man nodded and then smiled at her. "Welcome to the VIP section, ma'am. If Erik gives you any trouble, you just let me know and I'll break his nose for him. Again."

"I doubt that will be necessary, but thank you." She calculated there was a ninety-four percent chance the man was joking, so she mustered a quick smile.

"Any time you want to get back in the ring with me, you let me know. I still owe you for last time." Erik stalked past the ropes, gesturing her to follow.

The moment she stepped inside, the pounding beat of the music faded into the distance. "Sound dampeners?"

"Yeah. Just enough to be able to have a conversation without having to shout. I've seen you around here before and thought this might be a nice chance to get to know each other." He flashed her another smile.

"Did he really break your nose?" Some of the cyborgs, and even the Vardarians at the colony would spar with each other, but she hadn't expected to find the same combative elements here on the Drift.

"It was a lucky shot. I still won the match." He grinned. "But Dai claims he really won, because he drew first blood."

"And you're friends?"

"Good friends. The ring is just where we work, not where we live."

She could understand that. She'd had friends among the other cyborgs in her wing, even the ones that acted as their jailors and assisted in the experiments. They were acting under orders, commands none of them could resist. It hadn't been their fault. "I'm glad he didn't hurt you too much. I've seen some of those fights."

She suppressed a shiver. She didn't see the appeal of watching two beings inflict pain on each other. It reminded her of her former life.

"We rarely get seriously hurt. This is a sport, not a battleground, and it pays well, too."

"Well enough you can afford to buy a woman a drink whenever you want to." She hadn't meant for it to come out the way it did. Almost as if she were… jealous? What was that about? He could buy drinks for whoever he wanted.

He stopped and spun to face her. "Not really. In fact, this is a first for me."

"For me, too." She'd never accepted a man's offer to buy her a drink before. There'd been offers. Some for a lot more than just a drink. She'd always said no. That was something new for her, and she relished the power of being able to make her own choices.

He grinned. "Yeah? Then we should celebrate with something special. Would you mind if I ordered for us?"

"I wouldn't mind. I haven't tried anything other than the Torskian ale, yet."

Erik led her to a table at the back of the club. She worried for a moment he'd pick one near the windows, but he didn't. She picked a chair that put her back to the infinite expanse of stars outside and did her best to forget it was there.

"The ale is good, but we've got liquors from all over the galaxy and some of the best bartenders in the known universe." He sat down beside her and gestured for one of the waitstaff.

"Hey, Erik. What do you need?" The young man asked.

"Two star furies, and ask Luke to use the good stuff." He glanced at her, one blond brow raised in query. "You hungry?"

"A little." The truth was, she hadn't eaten yet today. Not that she needed to. Her nanotech would let her go for days without food, but it wasn't pleasant to go hungry. She hadn't needed to use currency until she'd arrived here, and earning it had proven more difficult than she'd expected. In fact, everything here had been more challenging. Food, clothing, shelter, all things she'd never had to consider before, were suddenly luxuries she struggled to obtain.

"Chocolate, cherry, or vanilla milkshake?" he asked her.

"What's cherry like?"

The server beamed. "It's delicious. Better than strawberry any day. If there's any left I'm going to snag another milkshake at the end of my shift."

"Could I have cherry? I mean, if there's some left."

"You got it." The man looked at Erik. "Chocolate for you, though. Right?"

"Right. And toss in some burgers and fries, too. On my tab."

"Coming right up."

"You're really buying me dinner just because I tripped someone?" In her experience, no one was this generous without expecting something in return. Not at Reamus, and definitely not out here on the Drift.

"The drink is for tripping him. The dinner is because I'm hungry and I thought you might be, too."

"Thank you." An unfamiliar sense of warmth filled her chest, and she found herself smiling.

"My pleasure."

"This part of the club is really nice." She sat back in her chair. It was better quality than the ones in the other areas. The fabrics were softer, and there was more padding. The tables looked nicer, too, and the floors were a polished grey tile that glowed with subtle swirls of blue light, making it easy to navigate the area. Every table had a light cube on it, set to produce just enough light to create a pleasant ambiance.

"Access to this part of the club is one of the perks of being staff. We're all allowed to take our breaks here if we want to, especially when we're working security. It keeps us on the floor in case of trouble."

"Does trouble happen often?" From what she'd seen, the Armas family didn't tolerate problems. Unruly patrons were quickly and quietly removed. They dealt with everyone fairly, but if someone caused problems, went after the staff, or broke the peace, they'd find themselves escorted out of the club by whatever means were necessary.

"Once or twice a night, someone drinks too much or takes more pharma than they can handle. Fight nights get a little rowdier. If you're staying for the fights, you're welcome to stay here in the VIP section. It's got a good view of the cage, they'll take any bets you want to make from your table, and no one will give you any problems."

"But you'll be back at work by then?"

He nodded. "Afraid so. Dai's fighting tonight, so I'll probably take over his post. I wouldn't be far if you wanted to stick around."

She was tempted to say yes, but she couldn't. If she stayed that late, she'd have no chance of getting a sleeping pod for the night. There were far more beings on the station than there were available beds, at least at the prices she could afford. And while her cybernetic enhancements made it possible for her to go without sleep for long periods, it had been days since she'd last slept.

"I'd like to, but I've got something I need to do later tonight. Thanks for the offer, though."

"Maybe another time."

She paused for a moment, sifting through the data and calculating the odds she was correct. Seventy-two percent. She'd have to clarify. "Are you asking me out?"

His answering grin was all the answer she needed. "That depends. If I did, would the answer be yes?"

The arrival of their drinks, both the cocktail and the milkshake, gave her a moment to consider her answer. She tried her milkshake first, and cooed in delight at the frosty sweetness. "This is good!"

"A woman after my own heart. You went for the ice cream over the alcohol."

"Doesn't everyone?"

Erik threw back his head and laughed, and a surge of longing coursed through her veins, sending her pulse racing. His appearance wasn't what she'd call classically handsome, but he had a rugged strength to him she liked. His laugh was warm and rich, like the topping on the hot fudge sundae she'd tried her first day on the Drift. And just like the sundae, she wanted more.

"You haven't answered my question, yet," he reminded her when his laughter stopped. "Would you like to go out with me?"

She nodded. "Yes, I would." Her plan to stay unnoticed had already crashed and cratered, but she still needed more information. Erik could be the source of that data. It was riskier, but she was running out of time. Eventually, word of a cyborg escapee from Liberty would reach even this distant outpost. Once that happened, she'd be caught within days.

If she didn't think the cyborgs of the Nova Club would help her, she'd have to move on. As she looked at Erik, she grudgingly added a new piece of unexpected data to her calculations.

She didn't want to go.

CHAPTER TWO

DINNER PASSED in a blur of light conversation, good food, and a surprising amount of laughter. Chance had a wicked sense of humor and a unique way of viewing Astek station and its occupants. He'd lived on the Drift for so long he'd forgotten how strange it had all been to him in the beginning. How strange, and how dangerous.

The fights had started, and the crowds were all packed in around the cage when Chance came by to say good night.

"I need to go. Thank you again for dinner and the drinks. You were right. The cocktail was a lot better than the ale." She grinned and added. "And the milkshake was amazing."

"Star furies are my favorite. Speaking of which, do you have any preferences about tomorrow night's menu?"

She shook her head. "No preferences. From what

I've seen, everything at the Nova is amazing. Everyone raves about the food here."

He noted that she didn't say she'd tried any of it herself, and if he thought about it, he'd never seen her eat while she was here. She always had the required two drinks to meet the minimum, but never more than that.

"I'll see you tomorrow. Be safe."

"You, too. No bruises before our date." She blushed as she said the last word.

Damn, he liked it when she did that. It was part of the aura of innocence that surrounded her, and he thought it was as sexy as hell.

"No bruises." He tapped his fist to his chest. "You have my word."

"Good." Her shy smile lit up the whole *fraxxing* room and his cock came to life with a surge of blood that almost left him lightheaded.

"See you tomorrow."

She vanished into the crowd a moment later, and he started counting down the minutes until their date tomorrow. He wasn't sure what he wanted to do, yet. But he planned on making it memorable.

It wasn't until he'd gone back to work and had time to think about their conversation that he realized she hadn't said anything about where she was staying or how long she was here. In fact, she hadn't told him much about herself at all. When he saw her again tomorrow, he'd make sure to keep the focus on her.

A few minutes later, his boss' voice rumbled in his

earpiece. "O'Neill. That pretty thing you had drinks with just left, and I think she's grown a tail."

A tail? None of the races he knew of had tails. It took him a second for his brain to catch on. Someone had followed Chance out of the bar.

He was on the move before he tapped his earpiece and replied. "Which way did she go, Kit? And who followed her?"

"Right turn when you get to the doors. And based on Toro's description, it might have been the guy from the starburst table earlier."

Veth. He should have expected the petty little jerk would be the kind to hold a grudge. "You got things covered in here?"

Kit growled in annoyance. "Of course. Go make sure your girl's alright. I've got money riding on the two of you and I don't like to lose."

"You too? Doesn't anyone have anything better to do around here?"

"Quit whining and move your ass."

Getting through the crowd took longer than he liked, but once he was clear he broke into a run. Kit had the door open for him, buying him a few extra seconds, and he burst out into the buzz of the station's main thoroughfare.

The concourse was full of the usual mix of off-duty workers looking for a good time and Corp-Sec officers out to make sure the fun didn't devolve into anything life-threateningly stupid. There were more than a few Intergalactic Armed Forces soldiers roaming around too, but that had become the norm of late. The IAF had recently increased their presence across the Drift, and it was causing friction between the soldiers and the inhabitants, who were used to being left to govern themselves.

He veered right and kept running, dodging around revelers and vendors hawking everything from food to footwear.

It didn't take long for him to spot her. She was retrieving a duffel bag from one of the banks of secure lockers that were scattered all around the station. Most of the businesses on the station didn't allow patrons to bring bags into their establishments, so the lockers were a necessity for anyone who was between jobs or didn't want to return to their berth every time they needed to change clothes. Many of the Drift's patrons were miners who worked for months on end, with only a few days of precious free time between contracts.

Once he had her in sight, he stopped running and started looking for the guy who had followed her. She was fine for the moment, and if he played this right, she wouldn't know about the danger until it was over.

It only took a few seconds to spot the asshole. He was less than thirty meters away, watching Chance with a feral expression that made Erik's stomach twist. The bastard was planning something, and it wouldn't involve pleasantries, conversation, or consent.

He circled around behind the other man, who was too far gone in his pharma-fried fantasies to notice him. He activated his comms again, keeping his voice to a low murmur. "Kit. I'm at locker bank nine-two-six. Can you send Corp-Sec my way? I'm going to need them to do a pick-up in about sixty seconds.

"They'll be there. Try not to get yourself arrested."

"That's not part of my plan." Getting arrested meant he wouldn't be around to check on Chance. Now that he was out of the club, he didn't plan on going back until he'd seen her safely to wherever she was staying.

He moved into position behind the nameless jerk and waited for him to make his move. It didn't take long. When Chance walked away from the bank of lockers, the asshole tried to follow. Erik didn't let that happen. He dropped his hand onto the guy's shoulder with a gentle tap. "You're not getting near her."

The man spun so fast he nearly toppled over, swatting at Erik's hand.

"Just wanna talk to her!"

"About what? Tell me. I'll pass along the message."

He glowered up at Erik, his eyes narrowing as recognition kicked in. "You! You battard," he slurred.

"Yep, I'm the battard that got you thrown out of the Nova," Erik deliberately repeated the man's mispronunciation. "By the way, you're banned for life now. We don't like it when assholes like you go after other guests."

He dodged a wild swing, grabbed the male by the collar and gave him a hard shake that rattled the other man's teeth. "I don't want to see you near her ever again. You hear me?"

"Bitch tripped me. Owe her for that."

Erik shook him again. "No. You don't. You need to forget about her. Hell, you need to forget about her, the

Nova, and this entire *fraxxing* level. There's a whole station for you to be an asshole in, but not here. You understand me?"

"*Fraxx* you." He took another swing at Erik, missing badly.

Erik abandoned speech and went for a more direct approach. He let go, stepped back, and waited. A second later, the idiot lunged at him, and this time Erik didn't hold back. He slammed his fist into the other man's face, stepped past him, and dropped him to the floor with a low kick across the back of his legs. The fool went down like someone had tripled the gravity.

"Stay. Away. From. Her." Erik ground out between clenched teeth, then backed away from the groaning, bleeding mess on the floor.

Corp-Sec appeared so quickly they had to have already been watching, and Erik made a mental note to thank Kit for arranging things that way. If they'd witnessed the fight, then everyone involved could state that the other man threw the first punch. Self-defence wasn't so much a legal defense as it was a way of life on the Drift, which meant he'd be free to go.

He knew both the men by name, so it was no issue to ask them to come by the club later for a statement. Right now, he had to find Chance and make sure she got to her place safe and sound.

She hadn't gone far. In fact, she was waiting for him, her bag slung over her shoulder as she watched him approach. It was the first time he'd seen her in full lighting, and the full force of her beauty hit him like a comet strike. Her eyes weren't light brown, they were a rich shade of amber, like honey held up to the sun. There was a dusting of dark freckles across the golden skin of her nose, adding to her youthful appearance.

"He wanted to hurt me." Her tone was perfectly level, a statement of fact, nothing more.

"You knew he was there?" If she'd known, why hadn't she done something? Asked one of the Corp-Sec officers for help?

"I calc – I figured it was possible he'd hold a grudge about the tripping thing. I didn't see him around when I left the club, though. I didn't realize he'd followed me until I reached the lockers. So many beings…" she gestured around them. "I'm not used to it yet."

"You should have said something. Told one of the Corp-Sec officers." He shook his head and corrected himself. "Sorry, no. I'm the one who works in security. I should have thought about it and made sure you got home okay." He offered her his arm. "But I'm going to do that now. Where are we going?"

She blinked in surprise. "Going?"

"I'd like to escort you back to your room and make sure you're safe. Corp-Sec will deal with the guy following you, but he might have friends around."

She looked down at his outstretched arm, then up at him. Her lower lip was caught between her teeth, her expression uncertain. "That's nice of you, but, you can't."

"You're sure?" Had she watched him take down the other man and decided she didn't want to go out with him tomorrow? Too violent? Too dangerous?

"That you can't walk me home? Yes." She sighed

and pointed down the concourse toward the section that offered sleep pod rentals. Every single one of them had a "No Vacancies" sign flashing. "I seem to be without a place to stay. At least until a vacancy opens."

He'd forgotten places like that even existed. Like most of the Nova's employees, he lived in the staff quarters that were part of the club. It was safe, clean, and cheaper than anything he could have found elsewhere on the station. "You're using the pods? Those aren't all that safe, you know."

"I know. But it's all I can afford."

There was no *fraxxing* way he was going to leave her to wander the station alone, looking for a safe place to sleep. He was the reason she hadn't won at the tables tonight. The least he could do was arrange for her to crash at the club for the night. There were spare rooms set aside for occasions like this. Decision made, he raised his arm again. "Come back to the club with me. It won't be the first time a patron has turned into an overnight guest."

"You're offering me a place to stay?"

"I am. It will be clean, safe, and comfortable. I promise."

She looked around, hefted her bag higher onto her shoulder, and then nodded. "Thank you. Yes."

He walked back to the club at a leisurely pace and noted with pleasure that she left her hand on his arm for the entire time. The night had worked out better than he'd hoped. With any luck, tomorrow would be even better.

This was not a good idea.

No matter how many times she ran the calculations, nothing she could think of improved the odds to an acceptable level of risk. She was smaller and weaker than the combat model cyborgs, which made it easier for her to pass as human, but any cyborg that took a closer look would recognize what she was.

So far, the cyborgs around the station hadn't noticed her because she didn't stand out in any real way. She kept the barcode on her wrist well hidden, and she'd dyed her hair so that it acted as a distraction, stopping casual observers from looking too closely at anything else.

They stopped at the door to the club to speak with one of the cyborgs that owned the Nova. "Kit, this is Chance. She's got no place to crash tonight. Chance, this is Kit Armas. He and his batch-siblings run this club."

"Hi. I believe I owe you a thank you for spotting the man following me earlier. I didn't see him. If you hadn't told Erik…" She had avoided running the calculations on the likely outcome. She didn't want to know.

"Taking care of our customers is club policy. I'm glad you're safe." Kit glanced at Erik. "I take it everything's been handled?"

"Beautifully. The troublemaker's in custody. Corp-Sec will be by later for our statements."

She stiffened. "Statements?"

"Nothing major. The officers saw the whole thing. You'll just need to confirm that the man who attacked me was the same one you'd seen in the gaming area tonight." Erik looked at her thoughtfully. "If you're tired, you could write up something to that effect and sign it, and I could just give it to them along with mine. You wouldn't even need to be there for that."

She nodded, grateful he'd given her a way out. She needed to stay off law enforcement's radar for as long as possible. "Thank you. That might be best. Too much excitement, not enough sleep."

Both men nodded in understanding. "Let's get you inside then. We'll talk to Cynder about a room, get that statement done, and you can rest." Erik glanced at Kit. "Can you let your sister know we're on our way to her office?"

"You got it."

Erik took the lead, and she was more than happy to follow him through the crowd inside. They reached a door next to the bar marked STAFF ONLY, and he paused to hold his hand over a scanner. The door opened, revealing a stretch of spotless hallway. The walls and floor were a utilitarian beige, with doors set into the walls here and there. A set of double doors with windows led to a large, noisy kitchen, but they were soon past it and a comfortable quiet settled in around them. It was the first time in days she hadn't been bombarded by constant noise.

Erik heard her sigh in relief and turned to smile at her. "Yeah. It's amazing how blissful the quiet can be after a few hours out there."

They walked for less than a minute before arriving at a door marked with Cynder's name. Erik waved a hand over the keypad on the outside, and a muffled chime sounded on the other side of the door.

"Come in," a woman's voice called to them.

She'd seen Cynder around the club but never been this close to her. The tall cyborg moved with the same predatory grace as most of the cyborgs she knew, a warrior born and bred.

Erik gestured for her to take a seat and claimed another chair for himself.

The office was simple, with minimal furnishings and an uncluttered layout. The only personal items were a collection of holo-pics that covered one wall. There were pictures of Cynder with her husbands, various staff members, her batch-siblings, and one that showed Cynder cradling two infants in her arms. The children had pale blue skin and silver eyes, and she was looking down at them with obvious affection.

"Hey, Cyn." Erik leaned back in his chair. "This is Chance. Chance, this is Cynder."

"Hello."

"Hello." Cyn leaned forward, her fingers steepled under her chin. "Kit says you need a place to stay tonight."

"It was Erik's suggestion. If that's not convenient, I understand. I can make other arrangements." Chance almost hoped Cynder said it wasn't possible. It would be safer.

"The hell you will. You're staying here." Erik shot a look at Cynder. "Right, Cyn?"

Cynder grinned. "That depends. Do you want to

stay here, or did Erik go into full protector mode and not give you a choice?"

"I did not," Erik grumbled, then glanced at her sheepishly. "Did I?"

She tried so hard not to laugh at the look on his face, but she couldn't stop herself. "You gave me a choice, but since you'd just beaten up someone who intended to hurt me, I'd say you were also being protective."

Cynder snorted with laughter. "I bet he was. Since you were technically still on duty, O'Neill, any injuries I need to make a note of?"

Erik raised his hand. "Just some bruising from punching the asshole in the face. I'm fine."

Guilt twisted her insides into knots. "You got hurt for me? You promised me no bruises!"

Erik looked sheepish for a second. "I know I did. If it helps, by the time our date starts the bruising will be gone. See? They're barely visible already." He held his hand out to her.

There was some redness and swelling but that was all. Still, no one had ever been hurt because of her before. She didn't like the way it felt. He was human, and they were fragile. He couldn't block pain or heal the way she could. She touched his swollen fingers carefully. "Doesn't that hurt?"

"Not really. I get banged up worse than this in the practice ring."

Cynder watched their exchange with interest, only speaking once she was sure they were done. "Speaking of reports, Kit mentioned you both need to write up statements for Corp-Sec." She handed Erik a data tablet, and pulled out a second one for herself. "You know the drill, O'Neill. Chance, if you want, I can help you with this. It won't take long, and then Erik can take you to your room."

She ran a quick calculation and couldn't see any reason why not. Plus, if she didn't handle the tablet, she wouldn't be tempted to scan the club's systems for information. It was an almost reflexive response to being near any computer, and the club's systems were well protected. If she slipped, she'd be detected, and no matter how many scenarios she ran, the results to that were never good. If they thought she'd tried to hack them, they'd never trust her. "I've never done one of these before. I'd appreciate the help."

"I've done so many I can fill them in with my eyes closed," Cynder said.

"Same here. This won't take long," Erik said, already tapping away on the tablet.

"Right. A couple of questions first, and then you tell me what happened, I'll write it up, and we sign your name at the end." Cynder looked down at the tablet. "Let's start with an easy one. Gender?"

"Female."

Cynder tapped the tablet. "Name?"

"Chance. Chance Smith." She'd picked the surname because it was relatively common. Cyborgs didn't have last names.

"Species?"

"Human."

"Serial number?"

The question came so casually Chance answered

without thinking. "Eight-two-nine-seven-four-seven —damn it."

Cynder gave her a small smile. "Sorry. Dirty trick."

"You were military?" Erik put down his tablet to look at her in surprise.

"That's not a military number," Cyn pointed out.

"You're right, it's not." There was no point in denying what she was, not when Cynder clearly already knew. "I'm a cyborg. What gave me away?"

Cynder shrugged. "Experience. You're not the first cyborg I've met trying to pass for an ordinary human. I've seen you around the club before. When you're focused on something you tend to become totally still. Humans can't do that. And I'm betting the cuff on your wrist is hiding a barcode."

She resisted the urge to fidget with the decorative cuff of cheap metal she'd bought for exactly that reason. She had no experience with subterfuge and only limited data on how to go about hiding her identity. She'd failed, which meant all her calculations on how long she could stay on the station were likely incorrect. They'd find her. Soon.

She got to her feet. "I should go."

Erik rose too, putting himself between her and the door. "Why?"

She didn't have an answer for that. She'd assumed they'd want her gone because she'd hidden the truth about who she was, which would mean she'd have to move on.

"You don't need to go anywhere. Does she, Cyn?"

Cynder shook her head. "If you need a room for the

night, you've got one. No one here is going to blame you for not admitting to what you are. It's easier to get by when everyone thinks you're just like them."

"It is. I--Uh--thank you," she stammered. For a split second she was tempted to tell them everything, but the risks were unacceptably high. There were still too many unknown variables. She needed more data and time to recalculate. She'd missed too many predictions already, if she messed up again, the best she could hope for was that she'd wind up back at the colony on Liberty. Just the thought of it tied her stomach into knots. She was never going back there. And that was the better option. If anyone else realized the extent of her abilities, she'd never be free again.

Erik didn't move until she turned around and sat down again. Then, he reclaimed his seat beside her, close enough their thighs were almost touching. "Cyborg, huh? So, I guess you could have handled that son of a starbeast all by yourself."

She couldn't tell them everything, but she could be at least partially honest about that. "No. I couldn't have. I don't know how to fight."

Both of them stared at her. "But you're a cyborg," Erik stated.

"I am. But I wasn't designed for combat. I was an experiment."

Cyn leaned forward, curious. "May I ask what your purpose was?"

She chose her words carefully. "Data analysis."

"That's...not very high tech," Erik said.

"It is the way I do it. I can absorb large amounts of

data, parse it, and extrapolate outcomes." She shrugged a little, as if it wasn't a big deal. "There are limits, of course, but it helps me get by." That last bit wasn't exactly a lie, but it came close. Given enough data, she could predict future events with ninety-eight-point-three percent accuracy. That wasn't much of a limitation.

Her ability was how she'd gotten away from Liberty and made her way to the Drift. She might have escaped from her creators, too, given enough time, but they had put her into cryo-sleep before she'd gathered enough data to do it.

"Brains instead of brawn. Interesting. Which corporation?"

"Primeon." It was a safe choice. That corporation had been defeated and almost obliterated near the end of the Resource Wars. Most of their records, including their cyborg registry, had been lost. There was no way anyone could verify her claim.

"So, you never saw combat?" Erik asked.

"I spent my entire life on a station until I was freed. I hadn't reached my full potential before the lab was shut down, though. That came later, after I was free."

Erik made a thoughtful noise and looked at her intently. "That's why you're so lucky at the gaming tables. You're running calculations and looking for moments when the odds are more favorable."

She nodded. "Yes, but it's a tricky thing. There are a lot of variables in play, and even if I get it all right, I can't win too much or someone will notice."

"And once they figured out you were a cyborg,

they'd toss you out. It happened to Jaeger all the time." Cynder shook her head. "Humans don't understand how we work. You're the only cyborg I've ever met that could actually cheat the system."

"So, if you tried to win big, you'd be thrown out," Erik said.

"And blacklisted. I'm already banned from two of the clubs on this station. I miscalculated and won too much, or too quickly. I've tried to limit my spending, but everything out here is so *fraxxing* expensive."

Erik's eyes narrowed. "So, dinner tonight. How long had it been since you'd last eaten?"

"Two days. But I'm a cyborg, remember? We don't have to eat that often."

"That's still too long. While you're staying here, you're on my tab. Eat whatever you want, I'll cover it."

Cyn just nodded, a tiny smile playing across her lips. "Or, if you'd rather not feel indebted to our knight in dented armor here, I can give you your own tab. It'll come due the end of the next pay cycle, which will give you a bit of time to get back on your feet."

Erik frowned. "My armor is not dented. My nose, yeah, but not my armor."

Cyn just laughed and picked up the data tablet. "I still say it's dented, but it's a good look on you. Now, how about we get these statements done? Fight nights are busy, and we should both get back on the floor soon."

Chance nodded, more grateful than she knew how to express. For the first time since leaving the Haven, she felt like she could relax a little. Maybe that's all she needed. Some rest, some food, and a chance to run a few more calculations. Then she'd know for certain what her next move would be. "Thank you both, so much."

Erik reached over to squeeze her hand for a brief but breathtaking second. "Helping people is what we do here. It's kind of turned into our calling."

Cynder just hummed in agreement, her eyes gleaming with pride. Chance looked at the other cyborg's expression and wondered if she'd ever have anything in her life that she could be that proud of. *Veth*, she hoped so.

CHAPTER THREE

Erik wasn't a morning person. That was one of the many reasons he lived on a space station. No sunrises. No annoying birds screeching outside the window. No officers coming by his cot to kick his ass out of bed at some obscene hour of the morning. There was only one reason he was awake this early in the day, and it wasn't the mug of *ja'kreesh* he'd already consumed, though he was fairly certain the Torskian beverage *was* the reason his heart was racing like he'd just run five kilometers in high gravity.

He'd showered, dumped several loads of dirty clothes into the laundry chute, and put in a request for the maintenance bots to be deployed to his quarters. While the bots went to work, he'd found a barbershop, one that actually employed sentient beings instead of an automated system, and got a haircut and a shave.

On the way back, he wandered into some of the shops along the concourse and spent some of his hard-earned prize money on new clothes and a few items for his date with Chance. He hadn't done the dating thing in a while, but as far as he knew, flowers were still in fashion. At least, that's what his married friends all seemed to rely on whenever they *fraxxed* up and had to apologize to the women in their lives.

He cradled the vase and bouquet in one arm, protecting the insanely expensive blooms against inadvertent crushing until he passed through the club and into the relative safety of the back area. He needed to get his purchases stashed in his room, and then he'd send a message to Chance and see if she wanted to join him for a bite to eat. It was shaping up to be a damned good day.

Cynder stepped out of her office as he passed by and whistled. "Holy *fraxx*, I barely recognized you."

"Got a date with Chance tonight." He nodded at the flowers he carried. "Do you think she'll like these?"

"I think you've been talking to my husbands." She smiled, but the expression didn't quite reach her eyes.

"And your batch-brothers. And the triplets. When they found out I had made contact, half the damned staff made sure to come by and give me dating advice. Never mind that I'm older than most of them and have been dating before you and your family even left your maturation tanks."

That drew a brief chuckle from Cynder. "Whatever you say, old-timer. Do you have a minute to talk security? Something new came across my desk this morning and you're going to want to see it."

That didn't bode well. He wasn't the head of

security. Hell, he'd only started picking up security work since Kit and Luke's twins had been born. The kids were special, the first children to be born with nanotech they had inherited from Zura, their mother. There were organizations that would pay an obscene amount of scrip for access to the girls, and the entire Nova family were committed to making sure that never happened. "Sure thing."

He followed Cynder back into her office and waited to hear whatever bad news she was about to launch into his orbit. It didn't take long. The moment he was seated she pushed a data tablet across her desk for him to look at.

"What am I looking at?" he asked, staring at the grainy image. It was badly pixelated and there where entire chunks missing, but he could make out part of the Nova's bar in the background.

"Our friends over at Nova Force intercepted a highly encrypted message two nights ago. Apparently there have been a few of them, but this is the first one they've been able to partially decrypt. Ensign Erben is still working on it, but once he got a look at these, he requested permission to give us a heads up."

He scrolled to the next image. It wasn't any better than the first one, but he could make out a few faces, all of them staff at the club, though there was one of a friend, Phylomenia Harrington, as well. The third was a little clearer—it was of the fight cage during a demonstration match Cynder and Toro had put on early in the week. Whoever had taken the shot had been by the railing, looking down on the combatants, and based on the view, they hadn't been in the VIP section.

"Someone's watching us." He set the tablet down on the desk and reached up to knead the sudden knot of tension that gathered at the back of his neck.

"And sending encrypted reports back to whoever hired them." Cynder tapped the tablet. "That match was only a few days ago. We're going through footage to see if we can spot our spy, but so far, nothing." She sighed. "But we do know one thing."

And here comes the bad news… "What's that?"

"She typed another command into the tablet and lifted it to show him the screen. It was an image of Chance inside the club. "This is from our security footage. Your new friend was here that night."

"Which doesn't mean she had anything to do with this. In fact, there's not a shred of evidence to indicate she did anything wrong."

Cyn held up a hand in an appeasing gesture. "I'm not saying she did. All I'm saying is that it's possible she's involved."

"And?" he managed to stop himself from snarling in frustration, but it was a near thing.

"And I want you to keep an eye on her. That's all. She's staying in the guest area, right? She doesn't have access to anywhere else in the club. I just need you to make sure she doesn't wander anywhere she shouldn't be."

"She won't."

Cynder nodded. "I know she won't, because you'll make sure that doesn't happen. I know this sucks vacuum, but we can't take any chances with the sprites."

"None of us are going to let anything happen to the twins, or anyone else. Like you said, we're family. And family protects its own."

"So, you understand why I need you to keep tabs on your girl?"

He grimaced. "Yeah. I understand. That doesn't mean I like it."

Cyn's body thrummed with tension and her eyes were shadowed with regret and grief. "But you'll do it?"

"You're afraid this is another Echo situation." Echo had been a cyborg employed at the club. A friend they'd all trusted. None of them had an inkling she was an assassin sent by their enemies until it was too late. They'd lost both Zale and Echo that day. Their deaths, and Echo's betrayal had cost everyone, but Cynder had taken it the hardest.

Cynder nodded, her eyes haunted, her expression hard. "I hired her. I trusted her. I will not be responsible for letting another threat anywhere near my family. So, I'll ask you again. Will you do this?"

"I'll do it. If I have my way, we're going to be spending the day together, anyway." His plan was simple. Spend time with Chance until they caught whoever was spying on them. She never needed to know anyone had their doubts about her. He sure as hell didn't.

"I thought your date wasn't until tonight?"

"If you had a limited time to get to know someone

before they have to decide whether or not to move on, would you limit yourself to one date a day?"

She threw up her hands. "Don't ask me. According to my husbands, I have no dating savvy and made their lives extremely difficult, when all I had to do was give in to the inevitable."

He thought about the way Cynder's courtship had unfolded. "You know, they might have a point."

Cyn's brows rose to her hairline. "I don't think you're in any position to be making statements like that, O'Neill. Not when you didn't even notice your date was a damned cyborg until I pointed it out."

"I was distracted by her wit and charm."

Cynder snorted. "You sure it wasn't her legs?"

"No comment."

"Smart man. Go find your girl and have a good time." She paused. "And I'm sorry I had to ask this of you."

He got to his feet and gathered up his things. "I get it. But when we catch the son of a starbeast that's really behind this crap, I expect you to make it up to her."

"You got it. And don't be sexist. Our spy might be the *daughter* of a starbeast."

He nodded. "Comm me if you need me."

"Only for an emergency," Cyn promised. "I'm letting the rest of the staff know about our potential problem in a meeting a little later. I'll need to tell a few people about my concerns about Chance, but I won't make it general knowledge. The family will need to know, though. And Phyl, too. She needs to know she's a possible target, and she's a good judge of character."

He nodded, unhappy at the whole situation. His friends were being threatened, again. It wasn't the first time, but it never got easier. Protecting them was part of what got him out of bed every morning. "We'll find the spy."

"We will."

"But it's not Chance," he stated firmly, and then gathered up his things and left Cynder's office.

He spent the rest of the walk to his room trying to figure out who their spy might be. There was a rogues' gallery of regulars, some friendly, others, a pain in the asteroid, but he didn't think it would be any of them. More likely to be someone who hadn't been around long, a vaguely familiar face in the crowd, someone who didn't attract attention. He growled in frustration. Chance fit every part of that description. No wonder Cyn wanted him to watch her.

"But it's not her," he muttered to himself as he opened the door to his room. The bots had done their work and scuttled off, leaving his place as clean as the day he'd moved in. He dumped the bags on the perfectly made bed, set the flowers down on the counter, and looked around in satisfaction. Not that he was planning on bringing Chance back here after one date. Hell, given Cynder's request, he couldn't bring Chance into this part of the club at all, but once the spy was caught...well. He was a firm believer in preparing for all contingencies.

He checked the flowers. For a small fee, the vendor had included a temporary stasis-generator that the Jeskyran swore would extend the blooms' lives for days, but he trusted cheap tech only slightly less than he trusted the average Jeskyran merchant. Which was about as far as he could toss a Nantari rhino.

He sent a message to Chance's room asking if she'd like to join him for a late breakfast, and got busy putting the rest of his plans into motion. He requisitioned one of the club's sim-pods and put in an order with the kitchen for a picnic-style meal. After the laughter and bad jokes about his dating life finally stopped, the crew agreed to have it ready for pick-up before the dinner rush hit. The Nova family were a pain in the ass sometimes, but they watched out for each other. Did Chance have anyone watching out for her? Something told him the answer was no. At least, not yet. If he had his way, that might be about to change.

LAST NIGHT MIGHT HAVE BEEN the best sleep of her life. She'd taken a gloriously hot shower in her own private sanitation cubby and fallen into her bed to snuggle down beneath clean, fluffy blankets. Warm, clean, and well-fed, she'd been asleep only seconds after her head touched the pillow.

She'd stayed in bed far longer than she should have, too, enjoying the fact she wasn't being rushed out of her sleeping pod so it could be sanitized before the next user. There was no duty roster with her name on it, no assignment to finish, no experiments to endure. This, she decided, was what freedom really felt like.

She took another shower, then spent some time with

the dye wand, touching up the red streaks in her hair, making sure that not a hint of white showed through. Her hair grew in white around the cerebral jacks and ports in her skull. She hadn't even known about her streaks until she'd been freed. The researchers had kept her head shaved to make it easier to plug her into the computers used to run her calculations.

It was a simple enough procedure to accelerate her hair growth, the med-techs at the colony had been happy to do it. They thought they were helping her fit in, not altering her appearance before she escaped.

She was still contemplating if she should put some of her clothing into the laundry chute for processing when a message arrived from Erik, asking if she wanted to meet up for a late breakfast. Despite having eaten last night, her stomach rumbled at the mere thought of food. Not because she was hungry, but because after years of consuming nothing but bland nutritional tabs, she had discovered a passion for real food. Walking the concourses had been a test of her willpower, tempting her to spend what scrip she had on the wide variety of food on offer from all over the galaxy.

She sent back a quick message affirming she'd meet him inside the club in five minutes. She donned one of her last clean outfits, tossed the rest of her clothes down the laundry chute, made sure she had the access card Cynder had given her last night, and headed out.

Erik was waiting for her right where he said he'd be. He was leaning up against the bar, a dark red shirt fitting snugly over the hard planes of his chest. His pants were charcoal grey and molded to his thighs in a way that made her eager to see if they fit just as well from the back. It was the first time she'd seen him in anything other than his club uniform, and while she liked him in blue, she decided she liked him even better in red.

"Good morning. You were definitely worth getting up early for," he greeted her.

"This is early for you? By my calculations, almost seventy-six percent of the population of this station is awake right now."

He gave her an amused look. "Seventy-six percent, huh?"

She shrugged. "Give or take. Most beings aren't nocturnal, and this is the station's day cycle."

"I'm not most beings. To borrow an old expression from my grandfather, I'm a night owl by nature."

"Isn't that an extinct bird from Earth?"

"They're extinct on Earth, but not the planet I'm from. The colonists used genetic material to clone the species as a means of controlling the indigenous rodent population." He grinned. "Apparently the little beasts ate everything the colonists tried to grow."

She wrinkled her nose in revulsion. "I hope the owls ate them all." It had quickly become apparent that while many of the cyborgs at Haven enjoyed spending time with the colony's livestock, Chance did not. They were noisy, demanding, and smelled bad. The planet's rodents were even worse. They had beady eyes, jagged teeth that could chew through almost anything, and a nasty habit of hissing at you from dark corners. She hated them.

"Not all of them, but enough that the colonists managed to survive. Cassien Delta is a fully developed world now, but it still has owls."

"And you grew up there?"

"I did. Haven't been back in…" He frowned in thought. "*Veth*. It's been more than ten years."

"You haven't been home in that long?" She understood that home was an important concept to many beings, regardless of their species. Some of the Vardarians living in the colony had expressed nostalgia for their homeworld, and there was always talk about making Liberty their new home.

Erik shrugged, and then gestured around the club. It might still be morning for the station, but the club already had a fair number of patrons. "Cassien D hasn't been my home for a long time. This place is my home, now. And these lunatics are my family."

He cocked his head to one side. "Would you like to stay here for our meal, or would you rather go somewhere new?"

"I'm happy to go anywhere you recommend. You must know all the best spots on the station." And she had enough scrip to enjoy one good meal before she'd have to hit the tables again. It wouldn't be at the Nova, though. Not now they knew what she could do.

"I might at that." He held out his hand to her. "Let's go find some fun."

She took his hand and nodded, not allowing herself to think too much or even start calculating all the ways this might go badly. As a friend of hers from Liberty had told her more than once that, a life without risk wasn't much of a life at all. Today, she'd try to do things the way Phaedra would - fearlessly. "Lead the way."

She'd downloaded every map and scrap of information she could find about Astek station, but that wasn't the same as experiencing it with a living guide. Erik shared details about the wildly varied collection of shops, bars, and vendors hawking their wares everywhere she looked. The noise and the press of the crowd jostling her usually made her uneasy, but today was different. She wasn't alone, and that made all the difference.

"And over there is Amped. It's a great live music venue. Some of the best talent in the galaxy performs there, but they never announce who is going to play on a given night. That way, no line-ups to give Corp-Sec conniptions. I can get us a table sometime if you'd like. I've worked security for them a time or two when they needed an extra body."

"Are you asking me on a second date before we've even had our first one?"

He raised their joined hands. "Or maybe this is our first one, and tonight's our second."

"Can you go on a breakfast date? Is that a real thing or are you making it up?"

"It's real if we say it's real. That's the nature of reality, sweetness."

She laughed. "I'm certain that's not how it works."

"Nothing is certain. Have you ever been one hundred percent certain about any outcome?"

She considered that. "Actually, no."

"And there we go. If you can't be certain of anything, no one can."

They reached one of the junctions that marked the different sectors of the station. There were beings everywhere, blue-skinned Pherans, towering Torskis, a few juvenile Jeskyrans with their first clusters of thorns proudly displayed. The junction was a transport hub, with a bullet train station on one side, and an entire bank of mag-levs.

She moved closer to Erik, noting that she wasn't the only one looking uneasy about the military presence. More than a few of the vendors and passers-by kept their heads down whenever the soldiers wandered past them. She knew exactly how they felt. She moved closer to Erik. "Busy place."

"It is. Those mag-levs carry hundreds of beings to the residential levels above and below the central decks. If this station was a city, this would be the heart of downtown." He pointed out various landmarks as they walked. "Over there is Corp-Sec's main office area. And down there is Astek Corporation's headquarters."

An argument broke out ahead of them. A group of civilians had crossed paths with a couple of IAF personnel, and insults were flying.

"Rock-grinding apes," a soldier called out.

"Know what IAF stands for? Ignorant Asshole Force," someone said, and another of the males burst out in drunken laughter.

One of the civilians shoved the nearest soldier, who retaliated with a right hook that sent the man staggering backward into a display of holo-cubes.

Lights and images flared to life, filling the area with a variety of holograms, most of them X-rated.

A woman snorted somewhere behind them. "So much for the IAF's legendary discipline. Archer needs to get his house in order."

Erik turned, then grinned. "Hiya, Phyl. If you plan on telling him that to his face, I'm going to need a ringside seat."

Chance turned and saw a lean woman with grey in her hair, hawkish features, and a warm smile.

"Oh, I'll tell him at some point. If the damned fool ever leaves his office." She gestured around them. "He needs to see what's happening out here. This isn't a *fraxxing* colony of peaceful farmers in need of protection. This is the Drift, and his people need to be smarter about how they go about their jobs." Phyl nodded to Chance in greeting, but before she could say anything the fight between the two groups reached a new level of hostility. She uttered a frustrated curse and held up a finger. "One second."

She placed her fingers to her lips and blasted out a whistle so shrill it set Chance's teeth on edge. "That is enough, boys! People are trying to live their lives here, take your playground antics somewhere else."

Both sides stopped fighting and some of them looking at Phyl with comically sheepish expressions. Chance just watched, fascinated. She'd never seen anything like it.

"But they…"

"Captain, you know we didn't mean…"

Excuses started to fly, and Phyl raised a hand.

"Edwards, get your crew back to your ship and sober them up. If you're not off this level in ten minutes, I'll be having a word with your captain, and then I'll tell Zura you and your boys aren't welcome at the Nova anymore."

One of the soldiers stiffened. "They threw the first punch. They're going up on charges—"

Phyl fixed the man with a chill look. "The hell they are. Do you know who I am?"

One of the soldiers nodded. "Yes, ma'am."

"Good. Then you know what will happen if you don't pay for the damaged goods and clean up this mess."

"You'll get us banned from the Nova Club."

"And then I'll have a chat with my old friend, Colonel Archer." She raised a dark grey brow. "Trust me, none of us want that to happen."

"No, ma'am."

"Glad to hear it."

Within a few seconds, the IAF soldiers were picking up holo-cubes, assisted by a grateful vendor and a few other helpful beings.

Eric waited until Phyl returned, then clapped a hand to her shoulder and chuckled. "You should have been a drill sergeant."

Phyl snorted. "Me in the military? Do you see me taking orders well, O'Neill?"

"Not really, no," he conceded, then turned to Chance. "Phyl, this is Chance. Chance, this is Captain Phylomenia Harrington. She runs cargo for Zura's shipping business."

She released Erik's hand and offered it to the older woman. "It's nice to meet you, Captain."

Phyl took it with a smile. "Nice to meet you, too. And call me Phyl. Captain's my job, not my name." She glanced over at Erik. "You're up early, today."

"We're on a date." Erik declared, reclaiming Chance's hand.

Phyl's brows raised. "Well, don't let me get in the way of romance. Not enough of that in this galaxy." She smiled again. "If you're with this one, then I'm sure I'll see you again, Chance. Have fun you two."

"Thank you. I plan on it."

They said goodbye, and Erik led her toward a cluster of food carts set up in the middle of the open area. "And here is where we find breakfast."

She looked around, slightly dazed by all the options. All of it looked and smelled tempting, but none of it was familiar. She'd been fed nothing but algae broth and food tabs at Reamus station, nutritionally balanced but far from appetizing fare. Food at the colony had been plentiful but relatively simple. Vat-produced proteins, frozen and freeze-dried produce, along with a variety of tubers for most meals. It had to be simple, because the colony was too new to be able to support itself. Even with rapid-growth crops and vat-grown livestock it would take time to get established.

"You look like a woman overwhelmed by too many choices. Shall I tell you what my favorites are and let you pick from them?"

"Good idea. Otherwise, I might need to stand here considering options until we both expire from hunger."

He laughed and drew her along with him. "This way."

They stopped in front of one of the carts. A Pheran male with tufted ears and deep blue skin tended a flat-topped grill covered with mince patties, while a female Pheran kneaded small balls of dough, then placed them into a tiny oven to bake. The savory scents of grilled meat, seasonings, and fresh-baked bread were as heady as the cocktail she'd had with Erik the night before. 'What's that?"

"Option number one. *Sheka*. Meat patties wrapped in *toral* loaf."

"The best in the sector," the male boasted, his Galactic Standard heavily accented but still understandable.

She replied in perfect Pheran. "Your confidence has convinced me. As has the delicious scent of your cooking."

The female turned to smile at her and answered in the same language. "My *vardo* is always confident, even when he should not be. But in this case, he is correct."

The male chuffed with laughter, his stripes darkening to almost black as he gave his mate a look of affection. "You will pay for that comment later, *vardi*."

The female laughed and went back to her work. Chance felt a brief pang of envy. She'd never experienced that kind of affection. She hadn't even known it existed until her time at the colony. Some of the Vardarians were mated, some even had families. It was also the first time she'd seen children.

"How spicy would you like your meal?" Erik asked.

She brushed aside her thoughts and returned her attention to the present. "How do you like it?"

There was no mistaking the flicker of heat in his gaze as his lips curved up into a wicked smile. "I am definitely a spicy kind of guy."

"Then I think we should go with what you like."

He reached up to stroke her cheek, his gaze locked on hers. "For now. But soon, I'm going to find out what you like. Spicy or sweet. Soft or hard. Slow, or fast. There's a lot I want to know about you, sweetness."

The only response she could manage was a weak, breathy, "oh."

"Exactly." Erik winked and turned to take their food from the vendor. By the time she could form words again, he'd already paid for their meal and had the packets tucked under his arm.

"Next stop, dessert. Then we'll go eat. Sound good?"

Her head was still spinning, and her thoughts were as scattered as a meteor shower, but she managed a nod.

"Great." He took her hand. "This way."

She had no idea what a strudel was, but they smelled divine and Erik had to like them, because he ordered four of the delicate pastries from a flirtatious human female who knew Erik by name.

"And two waters, please." She added, pressing in closer to Erik. When the pastries were wrapped, she handed over the scrip and claimed the parcel from the girl.

"Your hands are already full," she pointed out when he tried to protest.

He just grinned at her. "Yes, ma'am. Come on, I've got the perfect place for us to eat this feast."

She followed him to a small, unmarked stairwell across from the station and up a couple of flights of metal stairs. There were rust stains on the walls, the air was close, and there wasn't much light until they reached the top. It was an observation deck of some kind, apparently forgotten by most of the denizens of the station.

"Great views, no crowds. I thought you might like a little time away from the craziness." He inclined his head to the packed deck below. "You don't like crowds, do you?"

"I'm not used to them," she admitted. She didn't want to lie to him, but too much truth would give her away.

"Born on a ship, then?" He set out their meal as they talked, using the flat top of the barrier as a makeshift table.

"A station, but one much smaller than this. It was quiet. This place is never really quiet, is it?"

"Quiet? No. But you'll get used to it. There's something comforting about being surrounded by other beings. The noise. The smells. The energy. Now, I can't imagine living somewhere quiet."

Haven had been quiet, and because she'd stayed indoors, she'd often been alone. Despite the noise and the crowds, she preferred the station. Here, there were no open spaces, no wide expanses of sky. She shuddered. The open skies of Liberty had been difficult for the station-bred cyborgs to adjust to. Most of them had managed, eventually. She had not.

"There. Our feast awaits," he declared, picking up one of the *sheka* and handing it to her.

She took a bite and nearly moaned in sheer delight. "Delicious," she said around the mouthful of food.

"Glad you like it." He tore into his sandwich, and the two of them ate in companionable silence as they looked down over the bustle below.

Being with him made her feel safe. She didn't understand why that was, and if she was being honest, she didn't care. He was sexy, sweet, and protective of her in a way she'd never experienced before.

"How long are you planning on staying here?" he asked.

"I'm not sure. I think I want to stick around, but I haven't made up my mind yet."

"What's stopping you?"

She considered that as she finished the last bite of her meal. "I'm not sure it's safe for me to stay anywhere for long."

Erik stiffened. "Who's trying to hurt you? Why?"

"I can't tell you that. Not yet. It wouldn't be safe for either of us."

He blew out a frustrated breath and moved closer, his big body caging her in place. "I'm a big boy, Chance. I'm not worried about my safety. I'm worried about yours."

"I'm okay for now." She put a hand on his chest. "I promise. In fact, this is the safest I've felt in a very long time."

"You're not safe, though, sweetness. Not from this." He cupped her cheek in one strong hand and tipped her head up to look at him, then leaned down to brush a slow, gentle kiss to her mouth.

She closed her eyes and reached for him, arms tangling around his neck as she drew him down and kissed him back. He came willingly, his hard body pressing up against hers. His next kisses were harder, hotter, and more demanding. Her lips parted on a moan and she rocked her hips against him. She craved contact, the heavy press of muscle, the warmth of his skin, the stroke of his tongue as it tangled with hers.

He tore his lips from hers with a low groan and sucked in a breath as he stared down at her, hazel eyes almost glowing with desire. "I think I might be the one in danger here."

She let her hands slip from his neck to the broad expanse of his chest. She could feel his heart pounding beneath her fingers. It was beating almost as fast as hers. "I'm no threat to you. I promise."

"I'm not so sure about that." He covered her hand with his. "One kiss, and I already want you to stay. A few more kisses and I might start thinking all sorts of mad, dangerous things."

She giggled, and the fraction of her brain still trying to think rationally reacted with mortified horror at the sound. She ignored it. She'd go back to being rational later. "Who said anything about more kisses?"

His eyes narrowed a little. "Oh, there will be more. There's only one way you can stop them."

The last thing she wanted was to make him stop, but she couldn't help asking, anyway. "How's that?"

"Tell me no, walk away, and don't look back."

"What happens if I look back?"

"Then I'll take that to mean you're having second thoughts and come after you."

If anyone else had said that to her, she would consider it a threat. Coming from him, it was something else. A promise. She shivered and let herself sway deeper into his arms. "I'll remember that."

He leaned down, stopping a hair's breadth away from her lips. "Good." Then he kissed her again, and she felt the impact right down to her toes.

She curled her fingers into his shirt and clung to him as a storm of pure lust opened up and swallowed her whole. For the first time in her life, she stopped thinking and let herself *feel*. If today was all she had with Erik, then she wanted it to be memorable.

CHAPTER FOUR

THEY'D SPENT the entire day together, and Erik still hadn't had enough of Chance's company. He'd walked her to the door of her room and then kissed her breathless before letting her go inside to change. He even lingered outside her door for a few minutes, imagining her stripping out of her clothes, maybe taking a shower before their date. Hot water sluicing over bare skin… *Veth*. He had it bad.

Chance was a walking collection of contradictions. Analytical but passionate, wary yet impulsive, she had a head full of facts about the galaxy and everything in it, but she gave him the impression that life was all still new and wondrous to her. Being in her company made him feel like a jaded old man, but it also helped him see things with fresh eyes. Some of her wonder rubbed off on him, and it had led to one of the best days he'd had in years.

He took the elevator back to the main level, crossed

through several security doors, and finally made it to his room. It never ceased to amaze him how big the club was. Every useable meter of space had a price tag out here, and yet somehow the Armas family managed to pay for three levels of prime real estate. He'd asked Kit about it once. Luck, he'd told him. They'd signed on as one of the first businesses when the Drift was still an idea.

Erik hadn't arrived for another year. By that time, Astek station was coming into its own, a playground that catered to every vice and temptation in the known galaxy, and a few that had been invented right here. Vice was the reason he'd come out this far. He'd tried to drown his memories in booze, burn them out of his brain with pharma, and when that hadn't worked, he'd signed up as a cage fighter.

One by one, he sorted through the clothing he'd bought, tossing it onto the bed as he tried to figure out what to wear tonight. The bed was the same one he'd had since he'd started working for the Nova. This room was the first place of his own he'd had since leaving home for basic training. When he'd moved in, he hadn't planned on living here long. Hell, he hadn't planned on living, period, but somewhere along the line his plans had changed. Now, he couldn't imagine living anywhere else. This was his home, and the lunatics he worked with were his family. If Chance decided to stay, this could be her home, too. He could feel it.

It took longer than he would ever admit to finally pick an outfit. His date seemed like a great idea a few hours ago, but what the *fraxx* did a guy wear to a picnic? He finally settled on basic black pants, a shirt of black and silver *keski* silk, and polished black boots. He was tying back his hair when his comm went off with a cheerful double chirp. His friends in the kitchen had come through. *Perfect.*

With a carry-all of food in one hand and the vase full of flowers in the other, he ignored the wolf whistles and good-natured jibes that flew as he left the kitchen and made straight for Chance's room. He arrived thirty seconds early, but he didn't even have a chance to activate the chime before the door slid open.

"I thought you might be arriving about now." Chance stepped into the hall.

He opened his mouth to respond but forgot how to form words. She'd swapped her usual long-sleeved shirts for a sleeveless black vest that was held in place by two silver buttons down the front. Her hair was pinned up in some kind of gravity-defying twist that showed off the long lines of her neck, and she'd gone with a flowing skirt that fell just past her knees, the color somewhere between charcoal grey and black. He wanted to drop everything, haul her into his arms, and kiss every inch of bare skin he could find.

"Hello, legs," were the words that finally crawled out of his mouth.

Her lips quirked into a quick grin. "Hello, shoulders."

"Huh?"

"Oh, I thought we were greeting our favorite body parts." The smile turned wicked. "No?"

"You like my shoulders?" He'd had a lot of

compliments over the years, but usually it was about a body part a whole lot lower.

"You like my legs?" she dodged his question by asking one of her own.

One look at those long, luscious limbs had his cock hard enough to drill through the hull of a battlecruiser. "Hell, yes, I like your legs. Especially now I've seen them naked."

A delightful blush rose up her throat and stained her cheeks. "I'm not naked!"

"Your legs are. It's a good look for you." He winked and handed her the flowers he'd bought. "These are for you."

She stared at the bouquet of red and pink roses. "So many!" She took them with girlish glee and buried her face in the blooms, inhaling deeply. "They smell amazing! Where did you find flowers all the way out here?"

"It's amazing what you can find on this station if you know who to ask." He grinned. "I have a lot of married male friends. They know where to find the best flowers and chocolate for light-years."

She nuzzled the flowers again. "This is the first time anyone has given me flowers. Thank you. I'm going to put these away inside."

The dance of lustful thoughts dancing through his brain came to a sudden halt at her words. "First time? Sweetness, where the hell have you been that no one has ever given you flowers? That's first date one-oh-one."

She kept her head down and turned away, taking

the flowers into her room before answering. "I haven't been on a date before, either." She confessed once she was out of sight.

The door started to close, and he stuck a hand into the sensor space to stop it but didn't enter her room. "Never?" That didn't make any sense. Chance was beautiful, smart, and fascinating. Hell, he'd seen her turn down more than a few interested males just around the club.

She reappeared. "No dates. Not until today."

I'm her first. He'd never been anyone's first anything. "I wish you'd told me. I would have planned something grander for tonight."

"We're both dressed up, you brought flowers, and… whatever is in that container. This seems like a pretty good start to our date. I don't need grand, Erik. I just like spending time with you." She stepped out into the hall again.

"You look amazing, by the way. Did I mention that? Because you do. I don't remember seeing this outfit before."

She smoothed a hand over the vest. "Cynder and Phyl dropped by earlier. They wanted to see how I was doing, and Cynder offered to loan me something to wear. She said she knew how tough it could be to find clothes that fit when you're built to cyborg specs, and it's not like I can afford custom tailoring."

He wanted to believe that they'd only done it to be friendly, but he suspected they'd been checking up on her, too. Damn it, he hated this.

That's when he noticed she wasn't wearing the cuff

on her wrist. He took her hand, lifting it so he could brush a gentle kiss to the barcode imprinted on her inner wrist. "Beautiful."

He raised his head but didn't let go of her hand, only shifted his grip so their fingers were entwined. A sense of satisfaction bloomed deep in his chest at that simple connection. He was smitten. After all the times he'd laughed at his friends when they'd fallen for a woman, he knew the signs. He was in deep and getting deeper every *fraxxing* second.

She squeezed his hand and gifted him with a shy smile. "So, where are we going, shoulders?"

He laughed and led her down the hall. "I'm taking you and your lovely legs to dinner somewhere very special, and the only way to get there is by sim-pod."

SHE WAS WALKING a dangerous path right now, teetering on the jagged edge of the truth. She couldn't evade his questions much longer, and she didn't want to. Would he forgive her the half-truths and evasions once he knew the truth? She couldn't be sure. She didn't know Erik well enough to make that kind of calculation. Not yet.

She grounded herself in the here and now. She was with Erik. Holding his hand as they laughed and teased each other. It was going to be a good night. She liked the way he looked with his hair tied back from his face, and she couldn't be certain, but his clothes looked like they might be brand new.

More firsts. No male had ever tried to impress her, or even get to know her before taking what he wanted. Not the other cyborgs she'd been given to, nor the male staff at Reamus station. She'd been compelled to obey their commands, and that's all they'd needed from her —compliance. Erik was different.

"You've gone quiet." He slowed his pace to turn and glance over at her. "Everything alright?"

"More than alright. This is…" She decided to risk a little more truth. "I think this is the best day of my life."

He stopped, pivoted, and tugged her into his arms. He was grinning as he bowed his head until their lips almost touched. "Today was good. But if you stick with me, I'll make sure tomorrow is even better."

A delicious blend of delight and need filled her and she rose up to kiss him. "It's a date."

He growled low in his throat as he put down the carry-all and wrapped his arms around her waist, pulling her tight against his hard body. His mouth plundered hers, devouring her with a single-minded hunger that left her breathless. Desire tore through her, a firestorm that rivaled the heart of a star.

He walked her backward, pinning her against the wall of the corridor. His cock was a bar of steel pressed against her stomach, and his hands roamed over her body, caressing her everywhere he could reach. The heat of his touch contrasted with the chill of the metal at her back, and she arched into him, craving the warmth of his body.

When he finally lifted his mouth from hers, his breathing was as ragged and unsteady as her own. "We need to stop before someone comes along and catches us out here in the hall."

The thought of someone else seeing them together didn't bother her. Privacy was a relatively new experience for her. If he wanted to kiss her here, or anywhere on the station, she was all for it. "Is that a bad thing?"

His next words came out low and husky and his eyes almost glowed with desire. "Until today, I would have said yes. Now? *Fraxx* if I know."

He kissed her lightly, then straightened and moved away, freeing her from the wall. He picked up the carry-all from the floor and offered her his hand again. "But for the moment, I'm not in the mood to share. Come on, we're almost there."

She'd never used a sim-pod, though she understood the technology. Like several other businesses on the station, the club rented out the hard-light holographic projectors by the hour, offering the user a temporary escape from reality.

"Most of these are designed for a single user, but we recently reconfigured things and added a room large enough to allow a few users to use it at once." He grinned. "Or one Torski. Those big bastards can hardly move in the smaller pods."

"I can only imagine. Not much on these human-designed stations is really built to their scale."

He stopped outside a door marked 'Sim-Pod No. 5' and put his hand over a scanner. It whirred, beeped, and the red lights on the console all flashed green.

"Hello Erik O'Neill. Your program is loaded. Please

enter when ready. The program will begin at your command," the computer stated in a flat, generic voice.

"Will you close your eyes until we get inside? I'd like to surprise you with what I picked for a setting."

She nodded and closed her eyes, almost bouncing with anticipation. Would it be an elegant restaurant on another planet? A replica of a favorite place on his homeworld?

Erik took her hands and guided her forward several steps. "Ready?" He asked.

"Oh, yes."

"Computer, run program."

The silent room filled with sound, and her heart squeezed in panic as recognition hit. Oh no. She'd never thought…never even considered…

"You can open your eyes now."

She did, the scene around her hitting her like a physical blow. Wide blue skies. An ocean that stretched off to a distant horizon. Wind. Waves. Space. She scrunched her eyes shut again as a strangled moan of fear tore free of her too-tight throat.

"Whoa. What's wrong?"

"Sky," she managed to hiss the word past suddenly dry lips. "Too much."

He moved to her, enveloping her in a hug that helped to ground her. She pressed her face into the crook of his neck and focused all her senses on him. His strength. The warmth of his body. The subtly spicy scent of his skin. She tightened her hands into fists and squeezed as hard as she could. This wasn't real. It was a hologram. An illusion. It wasn't real.

"Computer, end program."

The room fell silent. Without the audio cues, some of her anxiety faded, though she still couldn't bring herself to open her eyes. Would he be laughing at her? Angry? Disappointed at her weakness? All the other cyborgs at the colony had worked through their fear, but not her. She'd been alone, isolated. Trapped by her terror and too screwed up to do anything but hide indoors.

"I'm sorry, sweetness. I should have remembered you were a station rat. I didn't think."

"You're not mad?"

His big hands stroked up and down her back in a soothing motion. "I'm not mad at you. At myself, yeah. I know a few folks raised on stations or ships, and none of them are fond of wide-open spaces. I should have known better."

She relaxed her hands and shook them until the feeling started to return. "I'm sorry I ruined our date."

"Hey, no. Nothing's ruined. You're here. I'm here. We still have dinner to eat. If you want to, that is."

She raised her head a little and managed a shaky nod, still feeling foolish. "I want to."

He turned his head to nuzzle her cheek. "Good. Right now, we're just standing in an empty room. It's safe to open your eyes if you're ready to."

"Does that mean you want me to let go of you?"

He chuckled, the rich sound rolling through her and easing more of her tension. "Hell, no. Hold onto me as long as you like. I just want you to feel comfortable."

"Still feeling too much like an idiot for that, but I'm getting there." She eased her eyes open slowly and looked over Erik's shoulder. The room was small and totally empty apart from the holographic projectors set into the walls, floor, and ceiling. *Much better.*

"You're not an idiot. Fear is a bitch with a long memory." He touched her face, guiding her gaze back to his. "I know that from experience."

"I bet you don't turn into a gibbering fool every time you walk into an open space, though."

"No, I don't. But if I see anything that looks even vaguely like a snake I lose my shit. It doesn't matter that I'm on a space station with a reptile population of zero. And yes, I checked."

"Snakes? Really?" She couldn't imagine Erik being afraid of anything.

He nodded. "My cousins dared me to go into the crawlspace under their house. Told me it was haunted and bet me I couldn't make it to the far wall and back without turning on a light. Turns out there weren't any ghosts, but there were a couple of dozen snakes under there." He shuddered. "I panicked, got myself turned around, and everywhere I went, there was another *fraxxing* snake."

"Your family did that to you? But they're family. They're supposed to protect you."

"Family only protects you from outsiders. Inside, you're on your own." He shrugged. "At least that's the way it was in my family. Which is why I don't visit anymore. What about you? Any batch-siblings?"

"None that I know of. I wasn't allowed much contact with any other cyborgs. My creators controlled what information I was given."

"So you're a loner, too." He eased his hold on her but didn't move away. "Want to be loners together?"

She liked that idea. "Yes."

"Good. Now that we've got that settled, shall we find another setting for dinner? Something cozy and indoors?"

"That sounds perfect."

"Computer, activate the most popular program you have with the following criteria: Indoor setting, no outdoor views, a venue for eating, romantic."

"Program selected," the computer stated a brief moment later.

"Want to close your eyes just in case I goofed again?"

It was tempting, but she shook her head in the negative. They were in a sim-pod in the middle of a space station. Nothing here was real but Erik. All she had to do was remember that. "I'd rather look at you."

"Alright then. Computer, run program."

She kept her gaze on Erik, who looked around and uttered a horrified groan. "*Fraxxing* hell. This is not what I had in mind."

They were standing by a collection of tables and chairs laid out for a meal, the white china and crystal gleaming against the dark red tablecloths. The air was thick with the sounds of passion, and once her eyes switched to low-light mode she discovered they were surrounded by holographic beings having sex in every position and combination imaginable, and some she had never even considered. She burst out laughing.

"Welcome to the collective depravity of the Nova's

clientele," Erik muttered, his face ablaze with color that rose right to the tips of his ears.

She couldn't stop laughing long enough to answer. It was unexpected and ridiculous, and she let the laughter carry away the last of her tension and anxiety.

"Computer, continue the program but delete all the holographic beings."

"Confirmed." The room was instantly emptied, and slow, pulsing music became audible.

"Sorry about that. Now that we're, uh, alone, do you think this setting works?"

She reached up to touch his cheek, guiding his gaze back to hers. "I think it's perfect. We can eat at one of the tables, then curl up on one of those nice lounges and talk." She pointed to one of the velvet-covered settees that had recently been vacated by a naked couple wrapped in an intriguing tangle of limbs. Some part of her wondered if Erik would be interested in trying to reproduce it at some point…

Heat flowed through her at the thought. She wanted that. Wanted him. Odds and risks flashed through her mind, but she ignored them all and took action instead. She rose up and kissed him, sliding her fingers from his cheek to his neck and pulling him in closer.

"Talk. Yeah. We could do that." His words were a silken whisper against her lips.

"Or we could…not talk," she suggested, hardly believing she'd spoken her wish out loud.

Erik's next kiss was accompanied by a low, primal groan of raw need. He rocked his hips against her and drew her into a slow, sensual dance, swaying to the music that filled the room. "Dinner now? Or dinner later?" He nipped her lower lip before letting his mouth drift from her lips to her throat, feathering kisses against her skin.

She shivered in delight and surrendered herself to the moment. "Later. Definitely later."

CHAPTER FIVE

HE'D *FRAXXED* up on a cosmic level tonight, but somehow, it had all worked out. Erik had no idea how he'd gotten so lucky, but he wasn't going to question it. Not right now, not when he had Chance, willing and eager, in his arms. There was just one more thing he needed to do. "Computer, lock the door."

"Door locked."

That done, he gathered her in close and swept her into a slow waltz that carried them across the floor to the chaise she'd pointed out. He wasn't one to let a good idea go to waste, and the thought of Chance's gorgeous body naked and laid out like a feast had his cock so hard it was about to punch a hole in his pants.

Chance had his shirt untucked before they reached the chaise, sliding her hands beneath the fabric to caress his flanks and back. *Veth,* he liked having her hands on him. Her fingers were strong, with faint callouses that spoke of hard work and commitment. Whatever she'd been doing before she came to the Drift, it hadn't been easy.

He kept kissing her, not willing to let her go long enough to undress. It made things challenging, but they managed, shedding their clothing piece by piece. They hindered each other as much as they helped, laughing as they kissed, fingers and tongues tangling.

She shrugged out of the vest, letting it fall to the floor before reaching between them, one hand coming to rest on his chest. Her fingers glided down his stomach, and further south, until she had the hard length of his dick in her hand. His balls ached and his cock throbbed as she stroked his length, exploring him slowly.

"*Fraxx*, that feels good," he muttered between kisses. His hands were busy, too. He stroked up her flank to capture one breast in his hand. She moaned into his mouth, the sound striking a chord deep inside him. Her bronze skin was warm under his hand, soft save for the hardened nub of her nipple that pressed against his palm.

He toyed with it, learning what she liked by the way she moved and shivered as he touched her. His cock twitched in her hand and she tightened her grip just enough to wring a groan from his lips.

He rolled his hips, grinding himself against her fingers as he kissed her again. She lifted her leg and wrapped it around his calf, her body arching into his, creating a delicious friction where their bodies met.

It took an act of raw will to end their kiss and release her, but it had to be done. He needed more of her than just her hand and her lips. "Lie down and let me look at you."

The corners of her mouth quirked up. "Should I salute before obeying that order, sir?"

"Hell, no. That wasn't a command. It was more of a uh…enthusiastic request."

Her kiss-swollen lips parted, and she laughed. "I've been ordered around most of my life, which makes me something of an expert. By my calculations, there's a ninety-six percent chance that was, in fact, a command." She stretched out on the chaise with a smirk. "So, I'm only doing this because it was my idea in the first place."

And just like that, she went from beautiful to irresistible. He toed off his shoes and shoved his pants to his ankles, kicking them away with a satisfied grunt before moving to kneel at her feet, his hands on her calves, coaxing her down the couch toward him. He parted her legs, drawing them over his shoulders so she was laid open to him. There was hard muscle under her soft skin, a subtle reminder that, despite her gentle demeanor, she was still a cyborg with strength, dexterity, and endurance that was more than a match for his. For once, he wouldn't need to be careful not to lose control. She could take everything he could give her, and more besides.

"Why are you smiling?" she asked, lifting her head to watch him.

"Because pleasing you, my glorious cyborg lover, is going to be a challenge." He grinned up at her. "And I dearly love a challenge." Thanks to the medi-bots he'd been injected with, he'd regained the stamina and recovery time of his youth, only this time, he had the experience to make it count.

Her eyes widened and her mouth went slack. "You want to…" she trailed off with a faint shake of her head.

"Please you. Make you scream with pleasure and keep going until neither of us has the energy to move." He ran his fingers up the inside of her thigh and then into the folds of her pussy. She gasped and arched her hips into the air, her eyes almost closing. "I want to see you come apart, sweetness. I want to hear your cries and watch you lose control."

Her reaction to his words was unmistakable. She gasped and gave him a hot-eyed look that could have melted the heatshields off a shuttlecraft. The scent of her arousal perfumed the air. He breathed it in and worked his fingers deeper into her sex until he found her clit and started circling it with his thumb. If other men hadn't given her the attention she deserved, then he'd be happy to show her what she'd been missing.

He flicked the pad of his thumb across her clit and she bit back a moan. "Don't do that. I don't want you to hide what you're feeling. I want to hear it. Your cries are music to my ears, sweetness, and I want to hear you sing."

"I don't…" she stopped talking and sank her teeth into her lower lip.

He didn't like the uncertainty he saw in her eyes. He wanted her happy, sassy, and moaning his name. "You do, now."

He placed an open-mouthed kiss against her inner

thigh before looking up at her again. "Whatever you want. It's your choice, sweetness. No judgment."

Her amber eyes glowed with understanding. "Whatever I want?"

"Anything." And he meant it. *Fraxxing* hell, he was in so much trouble.

She sucked in a quick breath. "Okay. Do it. Make me scream, Erik."

"As my lady wishes." He parted her pussy's lips with his fingers, then moved in to press his face against the slick folds. He zeroed in on her clit, sucking it into his mouth and lashing it with the tip of his tongue. Her hands dropped to the chaise, fingers sinking into the fabric until it tore, but she didn't utter a sound.

Challenge accepted.

CHANCE HEARD the tear of fabric and was briefly thankful that it was only a hologram she was destroying. Erik had barely touched her, but her control was already shredding. *Veth*, the things he could do with his mouth. She lifted her hips, grinding herself against his lips and tongue. He sucked on her clit again, pleasuring her with a single-minded focus. Her inner walls flexed, aching with the need to be filled, and he answered that need a second later, sliding two fingers into her channel and fucking her as he continued to tease and pleasure her by turns.

She moaned and was rewarded with a low hum of approval that vibrated through her clit and pushed her closer to the edge. She understood then. The louder she got, the more pleasure she'd receive. She closed her eyes, took a breath, and let go. For the first time in her existence, she surrendered control, trusting Erik with her pleasure.

She rode his mouth and fingers, crying out in wordless need as he took her higher than she'd ever been. Her blood sang, her heart raced, and every part of her was ablaze with desire as he pushed her to the brink. Her orgasm came on with the speed and force of a comet, bright, beautiful, and unstoppable.

She let her head fall back onto the couch with a shaky moan, her senses scrambled, and her limbs too heavy to stir.

"You are so damned sexy," Erik stated as he rose to his feet.

"So are you." She liked looking at him. The way he was built, the hard lines of muscle that moved beneath his skin like steel under silk. A few scars, long faded, marked his body, proof that life hadn't always been kind to him. He was strong, rough, and ready to fight, but he was also kind. Erik was amazing, and for now, at least, he was all hers.

He flashed her a cocky smile. "Glad you think so."

"I know so." She pushed herself up to a sitting position and tapped her temple. "I've run the calculations."

He laughed, a rich, rolling sound that filled her soul and made her want to laugh with him. He held out a hand and she took it, letting him help her to her feet before drawing her into his arms for a kiss so deep and delicious it made her toes curl.

"Top or bottom?" he asked when their kiss finally ended.

The question surprised her. "Pardon?"

Erik exhaled sharply. "*Veth*. Have you done this since you've been freed? I mean, you said you've never gone out on a date, but I know what it was like for cyborg women while you were controlled by the corporations. No choices."

She shook her head, a roiling surge of emotions making her throat tighten.

"So, you've never had a choice. About any of it." He feathered a gentle kiss to her brow. "And you chose me. I'm honored."

"And I'm very happy I did." She glanced down at the chaise. "The choice is mine?"

"Mhmm."

She recalled the way the holographic couple had been arranged and smiled. "Top."

"Good choice." He kissed her again, then crossed to the chaise and lay down. The rising curve of the furniture elevated his upper body so that he was almost sitting up. He held out a hand and crooked his finger to her. "Come here."

She didn't hesitate. She took his hand and let him guide her into position so her knees were on either side of his hips, the thick shaft of his cock trapped between their bodies. Once she was settled, he placed his hands on her hips and grinned up at her. "You are so damned perfect you take my breath away."

"Not yet, but I believe that's the plan." She rolled her hips, letting his cock slide between the slick lips of her pussy.

Erik's eyes closed and his lips parted with a low groan. "I like this plan."

She reached between them and moved the thick head of his cock into position. Erik tensed in anticipation, and she felt a rush of power as she held herself over him. He was waiting for *her*. Letting her take the lead. She shifted her weight and lowered herself onto him, enjoying the delicious pressure as their bodies joined. She hummed in ecstasy as her body gave way to his.

"Yesss," Erik hissed.

"Mmhmm." Her inner walls flexed around him, and her entire being was caught up in a shimmering flood of need.

"That's right. Take what you need."

She looked down and found him staring up at her with lust-filled eyes. "I need you."

He gave a playful buck of his hips, driving himself deeper inside her. "You have me."

She nodded, her eyes never leaving his as she started to move over him. His grip tightened, but he didn't take control, only held onto her as she found her rhythm. His cock stroked her with every move she made, filling her over and over.

She leaned over him, one hand braced beside his head, the other resting on his shoulder. A fresh surge of need hit, and she tightened her grip, her nails digging into his flesh enough to wring a low growl of need from him.

"Do that again." She loved the rough sound of his voice, deep with need and a hint of darkness that called to her.

"This?" She raked her nails down his chest. He growled again, hips thrusting hard enough to lift her into the air.

"Careful, lover," he warned her. "I'm on the edge."

"Noted." She leaned down to kiss the red marks she'd left on his skin. Then she gave in to a little darkness of her own and bit him.

He uttered an explosive breath, and the room spun around her. When her senses returned, she was looking up at Erik, who had her pinned beneath him, arms braced, teeth bared in a feral smile. "Sorry, sweetness, but I did warn you."

"I know you did." She twined her arms around his neck and her legs around his waist, and pulled herself up to kiss him.

His tongue thrust into her mouth at the same moment he drove his hips against hers. He fucked her hard, need building on need until she was swept away in a maelstrom of lust that threatened to set her soul on fire.

They drove each other ever higher, until at last, his thrusts grew uneven and his breath came out in ragged gasps. His cock swelled and then jerked inside her as he came, emptying himself into her with short, jerky thrusts, his mouth still melded to hers.

She teetered on the edge of orgasm, the release she

craved just out of reach until Erik shifted his weight and reached between, his fingers blazing a trail of fire down her body. He didn't stop until his fingers found the throbbing pearl of her clit, pressing it between his fingers with just enough force to bring her over.

She came with a soft cry, her senses shattered, thoughts scattered like the stars that filled the darkness beyond the station's walls. A comfortable warmth spread through her, weighing down her limbs and wrapping her brain in a pleasant fog she didn't want to leave.

Eric kissed her closed eyes and then moved off of her, somehow managing to settle his big body beside her on the chaise, his arms wrapping around her, drawing her up against his chest. She felt comfortable. Warm. Safe. She uttered a contented sigh and snuggled deeper into his arms.

"I know I should offer you dinner, or a chance to clean up, or something, but I'm not ready to let you go." His words were little more than a husky murmur just by her ear.

"Good. I'm not ready, either." She laid an arm over his and considered what she'd just said. She didn't want him to let her go. Not now, and maybe not ever. She started to calculate the odds of a future with him but had to stop when she realized she had no idea how to do the math. *Is there even a formula for falling in love?*

CHAPTER SIX

Erik strolled down the corridor of the Nova Club, whistling a cheery tune and trying not to grin. Three days. How could three days change everything?

Three men stepped out of the elevator and into the hall, all of them dressed in workout gear. Dai had a bruise blooming on his jaw, probably given to him by either Toro or Jaeger, the two cyborgs accompanying him.

"Still haven't learned how to block a punch, huh?" he asked Dai.

"Kick, actually," Toro drawled.

"We were working on some new moves for my next bout. You know, in the gym. You do remember the gym, right? Big room, lots of mats. Sometimes fighters go there to practice so they don't get their asses kicked in the ring." Dai grinned.

"I don't need to practice to kick your scrawny ass, Amari."

Toro chuckled. "I don't know about that. Dai managed to hold on for two rounds with Jaeger before he went down."

Erik gave a grudging nod of respect. Dai was straight-up human, which meant he had to be at the top of his game to stand up to a cyborg for long. Dai didn't even have the medi-bots Erik had. He'd declined the offer, the only one of the club's crew to do so.

Dai gave him a long look, scowling a little. "You're smiling. And whistling. *Fraxx*, you're damned near glowing. The rumors are true, then. You found a woman willing to overlook your impressive collection of flaws."

"Maybe." He grinned at his friend, not bothering to hide his happiness.

"Gah." Dai made a shooing motion. "Get away from me. For all I know that shit is contagious."

Jaeger clapped a hand on the smaller man's shoulder. "It's very contagious. First comes love…"

Toro gripped Dai's other shoulder. "Then comes marriage…"

Dai clapped his hands over his ears. "Nope. Not listening. Not going there. I'm a happy bachelor and I plan to stay that way." He shrugged out of their grips and started walking away, hands still over his ears. "I'm going to decontaminate myself with a very hot shower."

"Then comes Dai with a baby carriage!" Erik bellowed after him.

"I'm not listening!" Dai called back.

Toro and Jaeger burst out laughing.

"The harder they fight, the bigger the impact when they finally fall," Toro grinned at him. "I figure your crater will be big enough to hold this entire station."

Jaeger made a low whistling noise, then slammed a fist into an open hand with a dramatic "Kaboom."

"Haha. Really funny, especially coming from two guys who fell so hard and fast your wedding was accompanied by a sonic boom."

"True," Jaeger said.

"And totally worth it," Toro added.

"Which is why we wanted to tell you that when you inevitably screw this up, we'll be there for you. Women are complicated," Jager said.

"But we've got it figured out, now." Toro nodded sagely. "We're here for you."

Erik shook his head. "I'm good. I've learned a few things watching you and the others *fraxx* up."

Both men snorted and Toro bumped a fist to Erik's shoulder, nearly making him stagger. "Yeah, sure. We've heard that before. Like I said, when you screw up, we'll be there."

After a few more jokes at his expense, the pair of cyborgs headed off to their quarters to clean up and change before the club got busy and they'd both need to be out on the floor.

He'd worked a shift last night and would be back on the floor in a few hours, but before then he had lunch plans with Chance.

His comms chimed and he smiled. High on Chance's shopping list for the day had been a comm unit. He'd given her his code to program in once she got it. She was probably calling to let him know she was headed back to the club.

He checked the ID. It wasn't Chance. It was Cynder. "Hey Cyn. What can I do for you?"

"Is Chance with you?" Her words were clipped and there was a distrustful undertone that put him on the defensive. Chance wasn't the spy. He'd bet his life on it. Why couldn't the others see that?

"No, she's not. She's out shopping." He should have stopped there, but his mouth kept right on moving. "When are you going to stop looking at her like she's a bomb about to go off and treat her like a person instead of a potential threat?"

Cyn's next words were edged in ice. "She *is* a threat, O'Neill."

"The hell she is." He nearly snarled the response.

"I need to know where she is right now. It's important."

"And I need to know what makes you think she's a threat to anyone or anything. She can't even throw a decent punch! I know, I tried to show her a few moves so she could protect herself."

"She played you. She played all of us." Cyn snapped, frustration oozing from every word. "Dammit, Erik, I get it. I liked her too, but she's not who she said she was. Come to my office, I'll prove it to you."

Talons of doubt slashed across his heart, took hold, and squeezed until he could barely breathe. Had it all been an act? *Fraxx,* had he been that stupid?

He ground his teeth and broke into a jog, heading for Cynder's office. He didn't want to believe Chance had lied to him. He couldn't believe it. But—doubt tightened its grip on his heart—but he'd been wrong before.

He barrelled into Cynder's office less than a minute later. "I'm here. So, where's this supposed proof?" he demanded before the door even had time to close behind him.

Cynder gave him a hard look. "Throttle back the attitude. Now."

"You called my girlfriend a liar. I'm entitled to some attitude." He folded his arms across his chest, and forced himself to exhale before asking, "Show me this evidence…please."

She snorted and flicked out a hand, activating the holo-projector above her desk. "At least you tried."

He didn't answer. All his attention was on the projection. A number of images floated in the air. There were pictures of himself and the other staff, but this time there were more of Zura, Kit, and Luke. There was even one of the twins being carried by their fathers through the club after a doctor's appointment. It was rare for the babies to be taken outside the club, and he remembered it clearly. It had only been two days ago. During the time Chance had been staying at the club. *Fraxx.*

Cynder pointed to the images. "Our friend in Nova Force sent these over a little while ago. Our spy has been busy."

"And there's still no proof that Chance has anything

to do with this. These could have been taken by anyone at the club."

She flicked her hand again, and the images went sailing to the far side of her desk. "I know. But that's not all I have to show you."

A new image shimmered into existence in the middle of the space. It was written in Galactic Standard, with the information repeated in several other languages beneath. His gut twisted as he read what it said. It was an advisory to local authorities to be on the lookout for an escapee from the cyborg sanctuary on Liberty, and beneath the heavy lettering was a picture of Chance. She was thinner in the image, and her hair was shorter and streaked with white instead of red, but there was no doubt it was her.

"Escapee? That colony is supposed to be a sanctuary, not a prison."

"A sanctuary for cyborgs that are too unstable or dangerous to live anywhere else," Cynder pointed out. "That's why they were held in cryo-storage until an appropriate location could be found, remember?"

"Chance isn't dangerous."

Cynder's eyes narrowed. "Are you willing to bet our lives on that? What about the twins' lives? She escaped the colony, and instead of going into hiding she came here. Why? If you were on the run would you come to a place where you knew both the IAF and Nova Force were based? Hell, there are so many soldiers on this station it's making everyone twitchy. It's the last place someone would come if they were on the run. She's got to be here for a reason."

"We're all here for a reason, Cyn. This is the *fraxxing* Drift." He threw out his arms. "This is the ass-end of nowhere. Home to the lost, the broke, and the broken."

"She didn't just come to the Drift, though. She came here." Cyn stabbed a finger downward. "She came to Astek, to our club."

He didn't want to agree with her, but he saw Cyn's point. "Maybe she came here because she was looking for a safe place. We're not exactly lowkey about what we do here. We're the rebels who took on the corporations. The cyborg club where everyone is welcome. Why wouldn't she come here?"

Cyn scrubbed a hand through her short hair and sighed. "And what if she's a sleeper agent? Some kind of plant left by our enemies when they abandoned Reamus Research Station? She might be like Echo, an unwilling pawn, but that doesn't make her any less dangerous. I know it's not fair, but she has to go back where she came from."

His voice rose to a near-shout. "Back where she came from? Do you hear yourself? You're cyborgs. You don't *come* from anywhere. You and your family fought for everything you've got, and carved out a place for yourself even when no one wanted you around. Now you've got it, are you really going to start turning others away? What happened to 'helping people is our calling?' Cyn?"

"You know the answer to that. Echo happened." Cynder gestured tiredly to the images floating in the air between them, then crossed her arms across her stomach. "I hate this. I do. But I can't take risks when it comes to the sprites."

"Have you told anyone else about this?" If she had, then he was going to be fighting an uphill battle to get anyone to trust Chance. Hell, he wasn't sure *he* trusted her at the moment, but she deserved the opportunity to explain. Maybe there was a rational reason for her lies.

He clenched his hands at his sides. Chance had lied to him. *Veth*, that stung more than he wanted to admit.

Cyn was silent for a long moment. By the time she spoke, he already knew the answer. She had. "Once I knew she wasn't with you, I sent the others looking. She's not inside the club."

"I already told you that."

She met his gaze squarely, but there were shadows of regret in her green eyes. "I needed to be certain."

"So, now you don't trust me, either?" This day was sucking harder than a black hole in a vacuum.

"You know I do, but your judgment is compromised when it comes to Chance."

"So you sent your husbands and anyone else on your comm channel to see if she was hiding in the club. Which she wasn't." He turned away from Cynder. "Which means she's out shopping, exactly like I said. I'm going to find her and talk to her. If I think you need to hear her side of the story, I'll contact you."

"She's not going to make your lunch date, Erik."

He spun back to face her. "What have you done?"

"Vic and Ward are going to locate her and escort her to IAF headquarters."

"You sent a pair of *assassins* after my girlfriend?" His

tone had more sharp edges than a sack of combat knives, but he didn't moderate his words. He was too angry. Too *raw*.

"I sent two trusted friends to ensure a potential threat to our home was dealt with. She's being hunted, Erik. This is safer for her, too."

"*Fraxx* you, Cyn. You didn't even give her a chance to explain. She's no threat to anyone."

He stormed out of the room while Cynder called after him. He ignored her and broke into a run. He still wanted answers, but those could wait. He needed to get Chance someplace safe. Then they'd talk. He just hoped that he wasn't wrong about her. Being lied to hurt, but if she really was a threat... He pushed that thought away and ran faster. If he didn't get to her soon, he'd never know the truth.

CHANCE HAD TAKEN Erik's advice and done her shopping away from the main promenade. It was quieter, the shops and vendors more relaxed. Over the last few days, he'd taken her all over the station, showing her some of his favorite places. They'd listened to live music at Amped, gambled at some of the other clubs on the station, and he'd even taken her down into the depths of the lower levels to visit a sphere full of plants. It was part of the station's oxygen reclamation process, but its practical purpose didn't detract from its beauty. The air was damp and heavy with the scent of green, growing things. It reminded her of the colony, only without triggering her fear of open spaces.

She smiled at the memory of being in Erik's arms, surrounded by plants and flowers. He'd found so many places to take her while making sure she always felt safe. No observation decks, no tables near windows, he'd protected her every second they'd been together. It was time to tell him the truth. He'd more than earned it.

Her hands shook a little as she picked up one of the simple comm units he'd recommended. If he couldn't forgive her lies, she'd lose him. *Re'veth.* She'd lose everything.

"You lose your comms?" A male voice interrupted her thoughts. The tone was conversational, but there was steel beneath the words.

"Never owned one," she replied, turning to the source of the voice. It was Vic, one of the cyborgs from the Nova. She hadn't spoken more than a few words to him or his brother. They kept to themselves a lot, and both men gave off a vibe that she'd instinctively shied away from. They reminded her of the cyborgs at the colony, dangerous, potentially violent, and a little damaged.

A quick glance around the store revealed his twin, Ward, was standing near the store's entrance, trying and failing to look interested at the cheap electronics on display. Erik had been teaching her about situational awareness, and everything about this situation signaled danger.

"All these years and you never owned a communicator?" Vic tapped his temple with his index finger. "Cybernetic channels don't work over long distances. How do you keep in touch with anyone?"

She shrugged. "There wasn't anyone to stay connected to. Not until I came here."

"No one? It's been years since we were freed." Vic's amber eyes narrowed, and for the first time, she noticed they were the same color as hers. Her mind started running the numbers automatically, churning through data and calculating the odds. A second later she came to a startling conclusion. The genetic pool the cyborgs were created from had been small, all of it stolen from an IAF project called the Vault of the Fallen. Given that only five percent of the human race manifested amber eyes, that meant there was a ninety-five-point-nine percent chance that she shared a genetic bond with both Vic and Ward, who were batch brothers to Toro and Jaeger, Cynder's husbands. She blinked, stunned. They were her family. Or as close as a cyborg could get.

"No one. I've been on my own."

He shook his head. "Partial truths aren't going to save you this time. You've been alone, but not for years. You only escaped the cyborg colony on Liberty a few weeks ago, right?"

She tensed, every instinct screaming at her to run, but she didn't. There was no point.

"Don't even think about it. My brother is guarding the only exit. If you try to get past him, he'll drop you so fast you'll think the gravity plates malfunctioned."

She froze, and a tiny squeak of fear passed her lips before she could stop it.

Vic's brows rose, and the hard set of his jaw softened

just a little. "Holy *fraxx*." He breathed, his voice barely more than a whisper. "You're frightened."

She huffed in embarrassment. "I'd be stupid not to be."

His expression didn't change, but the lines around his eyes deepened for a brief second as if he were about to smile. "So, you're going to come with us without causing problems?"

She nodded. "Back to the club?" Not that she wanted to face the people she'd been lying to. If these two knew who she was, they all knew about her by now. But she wanted to see Erik again. To try and explain. She'd only just found Erik, the club, and maybe even kindred, but she was going to lose them all. Regret and pain tore through her, leaving ragged holes in her soul.

"Not the club. IAF HQ."

"I want to see Erik again. Please?"

Ward came over to join them, his hand still close to the blaster fastened to his hip, his expression hard. "He isn't going to want to see you."

Vic's head snapped up. "We could—"

Ward cut him off with a slash of his hand. "No time. We need to move."

Vic took the comm unit from her and set it back on the counter. She let it go without a fight. She wasn't going to need it, now. The only person she planned to use it to contact didn't want to hear from her. Tears scalded her eyes but she blinked them away, determined not to let anyone see her cry.

Vic took her arm in a firm grip and led her out of the store, while Ward took up position in front of them.

She went with them, her heart broken and her steps heavy. "If you see Erik. Will you tell him I'm sorry? Please?"

Vic glanced over at her. "What are you sorry for?"

"Lying. I didn't tell him where I was really from, or why I was here."

Ward's shoulders stiffened, then muttered, "We know why you're here. *They* sent you."

She shook her head, bewildered by both the accusation and Ward's hostility. "No one sent me. I mean, Phaedra mentioned that she had friends at the Nova Club, beings she trusted, but she never told me I should come here. She didn't even know I was planning to escape."

"Phaedra? You know Phaedra Kari?" Vic asked.

"Everyone on Liberty knows Phaedra." The fuschia-haired cyber-jockey turned princess was a common sight around the colony.

"And she told you about this place." Ward glanced back, his eyes hard. "Why would she do that?"

"She loves her new life, but I think she misses all of you. Talking about you was a way of keeping those memories close." She hadn't understood that before. She'd never had anyone to miss until now. But when they took her away from here, away from Erik, she'd cling to her memories of him and this place. They'd be all she had left.

"And she didn't know who she was talking to," Ward added grimly.

She managed a derisive snort. "This is Phae we're talking about. She knows everything about everything. Secrets are the bane of her existence. Plus, every cyborg in the colony is from the same place. We knew each other. Why would we lie to people who already knew the truth?"

"She's got a point, Wolf." Vic commented.

Ward just growled in response.

Vic sighed. "Forgive my brother. He's got trust issues."

"So do you, asshole."

"For what it's worth, I'm sorry I lied to everyone." If this was her last chance to apologize, she had to take it.

"Then why do it? If you weren't here to do harm, why lie?" Vic asked.

"Because I wasn't supposed to leave Haven, and I couldn't stay." She wrapped her free arm around her waist, hugging herself. She didn't want to go back.

"Why not?"

"Because she's afraid of open spaces." Erik appeared in front of them, blocking their path. "Hey, sweet thing. We really need to talk."

"Erik?" She took a step toward him, but Vic jerked her back to his side.

"Let go of her, Vic." Erik's words ended on a low snarl of warning.

"No can do. Archer is waiting for us to deliver her. You need to get out of the way, O'Neill." Vic stated.

"Move or I'll make you move," Ward said.

"No! Don't hurt him. Please. I'll go with you. I just want…" She sucked in a breath and looked at Erik. "I'm sorry. I should have told you. I was going to tell you tonight."

"You didn't trust me." The look he gave her was full of pain and wounded pride.

"I was afraid I'd be sent back to Haven. I don't want to go back. I can't…"

"I know. But you should have trusted me."

"She's a *fraxxing* spy, O'Neill. For *them*. You can't trust her. None of us can."

"I'm not!"

Ward shifted his stance so he could see her without turning his back on Erik. "You are. You've been taking pictures of the Nova staff and the babies. Sending them to the ones that control you." His voice dropped to a low hiss. "The Grey Men."

"What? No!" Her denial came out harsh and sharp, attracting the attention of several passersby.

"We've seen the images you sent. Don't bother lying about it, now."

"I'm a runaway, but I'm no spy." Her mind raced, automatically analyzing everything she knew and had seen around the club since she'd started visiting. It was too much data to sort through to be able to make any quick calculations, but maybe she'd find something that would help. It was the least she could do.

"If you're being controlled, you might not even know it." Ward stated, his tone flat.

"I'm not!"

Vic glanced around them and grunted. "We need to have this conversation somewhere else. We're attracting attention out here."

"Where she goes, I go." Erik folded his arms across his chest and stood his ground.

"Fine. Come with us," Ward jerked his head toward a bank of mag-levs. "This way."

Erik fell in beside her. "Trouble just follows you around, doesn't it?" he murmured to her as they walked.

"Sorry."

He glanced over at her, a hint of a smile quirking the corners of his mouth. "Don't be. How could I be your knight in shining armor if you didn't need to be rescued from time to time?"

The embers of hope she'd been nursing burst into flames at his words and she reached out to take his hand. "Thank—"

The rest of her words were lost in a blast of blinding light and noise that left her wondering how the hell this day could get any worse.

CHAPTER SEVEN

HE *FRAXXING* HATED STUN GRENADES. They always left him with a massive headache that lingered for hours. When he found the assholes who had tossed this one, he was going to make them regret it… just as soon as he could move again.

A prickling sensation washed over him and he gritted his teeth, bracing for the inevitable pain. The neurological stunners scrambled synapses as well as the senses, and the return to normal function was always damned uncomfortable.

The nano-tech proved its worth again, his medi-bots undoing the damage and disorientation so fast he only lost a few seconds. Ward and Vic were already moving, weapons drawn, scanning the crowd.

"Where's Chance?" He shouted over the ringing in his ears.

"They grabbed her and headed that way. Human

and two Jeskyrans," Ward yelled back, gesturing with his weapon toward the bank of mag-levs.

Son of a starbeast. If the bastards got onto the elevators, they'd have an almost insurmountable lead. He and the cyborgs wouldn't even know what level they were on.

"You're faster than me. Run them down. Go!" He barked the order in a commanding tone he hadn't used in years, but both men reacted to it automatically, their military training overriding everything else. They took off at a dead run, moving far faster than any human could have.

He grabbed his comms and hit one of the buttons, opening a channel to everyone he trusted. "This is O'Neill. A trio of unknown males have taken Chance and are heading for the mag-levs in sector nineteen, level five. Two Jeskyrans and one human. Vic and Ward are in pursuit, but we're going to need help to get her back. Respond if you can assist." He was getting her back, dammit, and he'd call in every favor he had to do it.

Answers flowed in from all over the station. Corp-Sec officers, IAF soldiers, Nova Force operatives, bouncers, fighters, and friends all chimed in. Within seconds, the mag-levs ceased functioning, security doors slammed shut, and a computerized voice started instructing everyone in earshot to take immediate shelter.

In no time at all, the concourse was empty except for the trio of males holding Chance. They were backed up against the doors of one of the mag-levs, their weapons all trained on Chance.

"One more step and we'll shoot her!" The human male called out.

Vic and Ward froze. They were only ten meters away from the suspects, hemming the would-be kidnappers in, weapons raised and ready to fire.

"If you kill her, you'll have lost your only bargaining chip," Ward pointed out in a conversational tone.

"Which will put you all in a really unpleasant place," Vic agreed.

Erik jogged over to the others. "You okay, sweet thing?"

Chance offered him a shaky smile. There was a bruise blooming on her cheek, but otherwise she appeared unhurt. "If I survive this, I really need you to give me more self-defence lessons."

The brothers blinked. "She doesn't know how to fight?" Ward blurted in confusion, never taking his eyes off the three men holding Chance.

"Not yet."

"For *fraxx* sake man, why not?" Vic demanded.

"Because she's not like you. She's not a threat, dammit. And I wanted to teach her, but

I wasn't allowed to bring her to the gym for training, since all of you had decided she was a potential threat," he snarled.

Chance's eyes widened and he immediately regretted his words. "A threat? Everyone thought I was dangerous?"

"Not everyone," he told her. "Not me."

Her soft lips lifted in a tiny smile. "Thank you."

"Oh for the love of sun sprites, I didn't sign up for this crap." The stocky human gripped Chance's shoulder and gave her a shake. "You, shut up." Then he looked at Erik, "And you, stop talking to my payday. There's a bounty on this one, and I'm going to cash in."

"The hell you are. She's a free citizen of the galaxy. You can't take her anywhere." If he could just keep them talking, there was a chance this could all end without bloodshed. Help was coming. He just needed to stall a little longer.

"I've got documentation that says different." The male muttered something to his two Jeskyran companions. It wasn't in Galactic Standard, but he didn't need to know the language to get the gist. Both yellow-skinned aliens straightened and gripped their weapons a little tighter. *Fraxx.*

"Then it's been falsified. You try and take her anywhere and you'll end up forfeiting your license," Erik replied.

The human sneered. "For what they're offering for this one, it would be worth it."

"Not an option," Vic stated flatly.

"Let her go and we can tell Corp-Sec this was all a misunderstanding. You can walk away," Erik knew there wasn't a snowball's chance in a supernova that Corp-Sec was going to let them go after they'd detonated a stunner in the middle of a public area, but maybe they didn't.

The human sneered, but neither of the aliens reacted at all. If they didn't speak Galactic Standard, it could be they had no idea they were involved in an illegal bounty retrieval. They were hired muscle, but he had no way to get through to them. He spoke a smattering of other languages, but everything he knew had to do with ordering food, weapons, or booze.

Good things cyborgs were programmed to speak every known language. He had no idea what Chance said to the aliens, the clicks and pops that punctuated her speech sounded more like static on a comm line, but it did the trick. Both Jeskyrians flushed to a remarkable shade of chartreuse, and an agitated conversation broke out between them and the human bounty hunter.

He risked a brief glance up. Two figures were descending down the mag-lev shafts, moving slowly to avoid attracting notice. He had no idea where Mack and Dash had acquired suspension belts, but he was glad they had them. They silently dropped into position behind the suspects while the trio was distracted.

Ward held a hand behind his back where Erik could see it and started counting down on his fingers. Three. Two. One.

The doors opened behind the suspects as Vic and Ward raised their weapons.

"Freeze!" Someone bellowed.

"Chance, down!" He yelled. He didn't want her getting caught by a stray shot if things went to hell.

He kept his gaze locked on her, ignoring everything else, willing her to hear him. She did.

She dropped to the ground almost instantly, using gravity to break her captor's hold. She curled into a ball, arms protecting her head, and he winced as one of the Jeskyran's pivoted and tried to run, inadvertently slamming a cluster of thorns into her calf.

Her only reaction was to curl into a smaller ball, and a flash of pride shot through him. She had to be terrified, but she'd kept her head, distracted the enemy, and done her best to get out of the way. She might not be trained for combat, but she had courage to spare.

A blaster fired and a hail of red and blue bolts sizzled through the air, painting Chance in a flash of colors that faded as quickly as they'd appeared. He looked up in time to see the human bounty hunter stagger and then tumble to the deck, narrowly missing Chance.

"You're slowing down," Vic taunted Ward.

"Like hell. My first shot hit before you even pulled the trigger," his brother retorted as he lowered his weapon.

"In your dreams."

"Want to watch the replay?"

"Got my own, thanks."

"You two need therapy," he muttered, striding past them to get to Chance.

"You have no idea how much," Ward said softly.

Any other day, he'd have followed up on that statement, but not today. He dropped into a crouch at her side, one hand landing lightly on her shoulder. "Hey, there, sweet thing. Come here often?"

She uttered a muffled snort of laughter and eased her arms down from over her head, then looked up at him. "I cannot believe you said that."

"I was trying to make you smile. Did it work?"

She uttered a soft, pleased noise and rose, almost throwing herself into his arms. She wrapped shaking hands around his neck, buried her face against his shoulder, and held on like she would never let him go. "You came to find me. You didn't let them take me. They said… I thought…"

He curled his body around hers and breathed in her scent, letting it soothe the ragged edges of his soul. "I will always come for you. If you need me, I'll be there."

"But I lied to you."

He stroked her hair, skimming lightly over the cranial ports hidden beneath the silken warmth. "Yeah, and we're going to talk about that. And then you are going to swear to me that you're never going to lie to me about anything, ever again."

"Never," she agreed.

"Okay then. Glad we got that settled."

Booted feet surrounded them. "Sir. You need to release the prisoner, now."

He looked up. There were a half-dozen armed men and women in IAF uniforms standing in a ring around them, and not one of them looked friendly.

"She's not a prisoner, she's a *fraxxing* victim. Those three males tried to abduct her. Deal with them, I'll take care of her."

"No, sir. Corp-Sec is investigating the bounty hunters. We're here for her."

"On whose authority?" He demanded.

"Colonel Scott Archer."

Fraxx. "Why does the local head of the Intergalactic Armed Forces want to talk to the victim of a kidnapping?" He looked around at the soldiers and got nothing but perfectly blank expressions. "Never mind, I can see you don't know the answer to that question."

That garnered him a couple of frowns. "Sir?"

"I know that look. It's the IAF's standard-issue expression when you're asked a question above your paygrade." He waved them off. "Stand back. I'm going to help my girlfriend to her feet. Then someone is going to treat her injuries. While that happens, you can let the Colonel know that if he would like to speak to Chance, he can come here and do it. She's been attacked and injured and she's not going anywhere right now. We clear, Corporal?"

He put enough command in his tone that the younger man started to salute, then froze, his hand suspended in the air as if he didn't know what to do with it. "Sir yes…uh… sir. I'll advise the Colonel of the situation."

"Good." He ignored the soldier's confusion and gently unwrapped Chance's arms. "How's the leg? You okay to stand up?"

"It's' fine." She let go of him reluctantly. "Cyborg, remember? Medi-bots and the ability to temporarily block out pain." She let him help her to her feet, then stepped in close and kissed him. "Thank you for coming for me."

"Always." It surprised him how easily he made that promise. A week ago, she'd been nothing more than a pretty face in the crowd. Now? He smiled down at her beautiful face. Now, she was the brightest star in his sky.

As requested, one of the soldiers retrieved a first aid kit and treated her injured leg. It didn't take long, but he knew from experience that wounds from Jeskyrian body thorns could be deeper than they looked and prone to infection. Medi-bots or not, he wasn't taking any risks. Besides, the longer they stayed here, the more of his friends and allies arrived. He was going to need them all for what came next. He wasn't letting them take Chance. Once they had her, she'd be on a ship back to Haven and out of reach in a nanosecond or three.

Mack and Dash had taken over the scene, directing other Corp-Sec officers as they gathered evidence and witness statements. A crowd gathered while they worked, until there was a throng of beings standing outside the holographic barriers that marked the perimeter. He recognized every single one of them. Archer might have the IAF, but he had an army of his own. He was done following other people's orders. Chance wasn't going anywhere without him. Ever.

CHANCE DIDN'T UNDERSTAND EXACTLY what had happened, but the more she listened to the conversations around her, the more data she compiled. Despite the way things had started out, Vic and Ward appeared to be on her side, now. They stood guard a few feet to either side of her, keeping a wary eye on the medic treating her leg. Erik hadn't left her alone for even a second. He stayed in constant contact, never letting go of her hand. She hadn't known any of her attackers, a fact she'd had to repeat more than once to the Corp-Sec officers who came and went, asking questions and confirming details.

When the bustle started to subside, she turned to Erik and Dash, one of the officers who had taken part in her rescue. It was time to verify a few of her theories. "Who were those three who grabbed me?"

"Bounty hunters. The two Jeskyrians had full certifications, but the human had been suspended for multiple violations. From what the two survivors told us, the human was in charge, and he wasn't forthcoming about the details of the mission or his current status. He even met their local contact without them. All they knew was where the meeting was." Dash's jaw flexed. "It was at the Nova Club."

"Son of a bitch. That was arrogant of them," Erik growled.

She added that tidbit of information to her calculations. Every bit of data helped her narrow down the list of potential suspects. "I still don't understand why someone would take out a black-market contract on me.

"Because they know what you can do, baby." Erik moved closer to her, his hand tightening on hers. "That amazing brain of yours could be used as a weapon. My guess is someone wants you in their arsenal."

"That doesn't make sense. If I had any value, I wouldn't have been left behind when they abandoned Reamus station."

Eric growled. "You have value. Don't you ever say otherwise or I will tan your pretty ass pink."

She blushed and glanced at Dash, who shook his head. "Don't mind me. I've got selective hearing, and I definitely didn't hear what he just said."

"What?" Erik asked.

Dash just chuckled. "I'm starting to see why you've been single so long."

Erik flicked his fingers out in a rude gesture and then turned back to her. "Someone must know what you can do."

Dash frowned. "Uh. What can you do?"

She felt a sharp stab of fear at his question. This was the moment she'd been dreading. She took a breath and hung onto Erik's hand. "Given enough data, I can predict future events to an extremely high level of accuracy."

Dash cocked his head, blue-gray eyes curious. "So can several AI programs I can think of. Why target you?"

"Because given enough data, my calculations have an accuracy of ninety-eight-point-three percent. That's almost five percent higher than even the best AI."

Dash whistled.

Erik stared at her. "I knew you were gifted, but damn, that high? Really? That's *fraxxing* incredible… and you didn't tell me."

"It was on the list of things I needed to tell you today."

"List, huh? How long is this list?" His tone was teasing, but that didn't stop her from feeling a twisting stab of guilt. She should have trusted him sooner.

"Not that long, really. You already know I'm one of

the refugees from Reamus research labs. I was created after the war ended, and I was only freed of my conditioning after I was roused from my cryo-pod once we made it to the colony on Liberty."

"You were created *after* the war?" Erik repeated. "*Veth*, I knew you were younger than me, but that's a hell of an age gap."

"You're worried about my age? Why? I wasn't born, I came out of a maturation vat as a fully formed adult, just like every other cyborg you know. Age is not relevant to us."

He winked at her. "I know, but that's not going to stop some people from thinking I'm robbing the cradle."

"If anyone says anything, tell them I never had a cradle." She frowned as a thought hit her. "I won't age, Erik. No one knows how long cyborgs will live, but it's a long time. Is the age thing going to be a problem?"

Dash made a soft choking noise. "You didn't tell her?"

"Don't you have a crime scene to investigate? Witnesses to talk to?" Erik made a shooing motion with his free hand.

"That's what I'm doing. I just learned about a motive for the attempted kidnapping. Who knows what else I might learn if I stick around?"

"What didn't you tell me?" she asked, ignoring the byplay between the men. If Erik had been keeping secrets, too, that might help rebalance the scales between them.

He looked around, but no one was near them at the moment. "You're not the only one with nanotech."

"What? How?" She only knew of one human who carried that kind of technology - Phaedra. But she carried her husbands' Vardarian tech, not something designed by humans. At least... that's what she'd assumed.

"Long story. I'll tell you about it once we're back at the club."

She looked around them. They were still surrounded by armed soldiers, and while Dash and some of the other Corp-Sec officers were permitted to approach, no one else had been able to. She wasn't sure she was going back to the Nova Club, now, or ever again.

He must have understood her worry, because he lifted her hand to his mouth and kissed her fingers, just the same as the night they'd first spoken. "If you want to stay here, we'll find a way to make that happen. I promise."

"What if the others don't believe I'm not the spy?"

"The others?" he threw out a hand to encompass the crowd standing beyond the soldiers. "You mean them? They're here because I asked them to help you. Every single one of them. If they really believed you were a threat, they wouldn't have come."

She looked again, this time taking time to register the faces and identities of everyone there. She couldn't see everyone, but she didn't need to. She started comparing the names of those present to potential suspects, and within seconds she had the answer. "I know who it is."

"Slow down. You know what?" Erik asked.

"The spy." She touched her temple. "Ninety-six percent surety. You gave me the missing piece of the puzzle.

He moved in closer and dropped his voice to a low whisper. "Who is it?"

"It has to be Kirk. The dealer from the starburst table the night we met."

"What makes you think that?" Erik asked, then frowned and added. "Not that I doubt you. I want to hear your reasons so I can explain to the others."

"He's a newer hire, right? And he's always looking for ways to make bigger tips, like moving up to the starburst table when he didn't have permission, and letting intoxicated players keep betting if they were good tippers. He was working extra shifts, too. I noticed that he was around almost every night. He needed money. Plus, that bounty hunter met with someone at the club. Whoever Kirk was reporting to, he must have told them about me. They used him as their contact point for the hunters."

Erik nodded. "Makes sense. We'll have to check the security footage and see if the bounty hunter met with him. That would prove everything nicely."

"Already happening. Cyn sent the files over to Corp-Sec and my people are scanning it with facial-rec software to find the bounty hunter," Dash said, his voice as low as theirs.

"There's something else," she added and gestured to

the crowd. "He's not here. This place is full of club employees and friends, but not him. Odds are good he heard Erik's call for help and realized things were falling out of orbit. He's probably trying to find a way off the station."

"That's not going to happen." Dash didn't move, but his eyes went distant for a moment, and she knew he was communicating to other cyborgs via their internal channel.

She'd never been linked to others that way. Never had friends to rely on, or anyone to reach out to. She looked around again. Erik had asked for help, and all these beings had dropped everything to answer. It was a testament to the kind of man he was, and the quality of his friends.

No, not friends. *Family*.

Her eyes slid to the cloned twins, Vic and Ward. Family. She had some, now. They were batch brothers to Cynder's husbands, which meant they were her family, too. Not that she was telling them. Not yet. This wasn't the place, or the time.

"Message relayed. He's not getting off the station unless he takes a deep breath and throws himself out an airlock," Dash reported a few seconds later.

"If Jaeger or Cyn get a hold of him, he'll probably wish he'd done just that," Erik looked like he'd happily throw Kirk out an airlock himself, but none of his anger was directed at her.

The crowd around them stirred and a sense of tension filled the space. One by one the conversations faded until there was barely a whisper of sound.

"Can someone tell me why the *fraxx* my soldiers are reporting a hostile crowd are preventing them from fulfilling their orders?" A voice boomed into the silence.

"Whatever happens, you stay close to me." Erik kissed her cheek, gave her hand a tight squeeze, then raised his head and called out, "Because you ordered them to take our friend into custody, and she's done nothing wrong. If you want Chance, you'll have to take her by force. Isn't that right, guys?"

"Right!" The answer came back on a thunderous chorus.

Something broke deep inside her, and there were tears on her cheeks as she realized that this was what she'd been missing. *This* was what it was like to belong. Her heart clenched. This was everything she wanted, but she knew the odds. It wasn't likely to be hers for long.

CHAPTER EIGHT

HE DIDN'T WANT to do it, but Erik let go of Chance's hand and stepped forward, putting himself between her and Archer. He wasn't sure how the *fraxx* he was going to make this work, but he'd find a way. If he didn't, then he'd be on a ship to the colony on Liberty, because there was no way in hell he was letting Chance slip away from him.

The crowd parted and Colonel Scott Archer walked into view. He was a big man with a powerful build, and while there was silver in his hair, there was no doubt he was still a man in his prime. His uniform was perfect, every crease straight, every button gleaming as bright as the polish on his boots.

"Lieutenant Commander O'Neill. Care to explain to me what the hell is going on here?"

Erik ignored the universal look of shock on the faces of his friends. He never spoke about his past. It brought up memories he preferred to keep buried, and Archer had to know it.

He drew himself up to his full height and met the colonel's gaze. "Which part, sir?"

Archer's jaw tightened. "Let's start with why that cyborg is still walking around the station when she should be in IAF custody."

"Because she's a free citizen of the galaxy and she's done nothing wrong."

"And she wants to stay here, with Erik," Chance chimed in.

He was tempted to turn around and kiss her. With all the chaos, they hadn't talked about future plans. He knew she didn't want to go back to the colony, but staying with him was something else entirely. Something permanent, and…right.

"You can't stay here," Archer stated, his tone firm.

"Why not?" Erik demanded.

"Because we have an agreement in place with the cyborgs of that colony. The rules were agreed to by both sides and put in place to protect everyone."

"I didn't agree to anything. I woke up in a strange place and was told I couldn't leave. Ever." Chance said, her voice pitched loud enough to carry.

There was a general stir of muttered conversation. Not many knew the details of the agreement. It hadn't occurred to most of them that the cyborgs living there would never be allowed to leave the planet, and those who knew weren't supposed to talk about it.

Archer's expression didn't change. "A designated representative from your group made the deal on your behalf. That doesn't change the fact you are expected to abide by it. If you don't, you could jeopardize the entire agreement." He spread his hands in a placating gesture. "I don't make the rules, I just enforce them."

A new voice rang out. "Dammit, Archer. Don't you ever get tired of following the rules? Especially when you know they're wrong?"

Phylomenia Harrington, captain of the cargo ship the *Beacon,* and unofficial den mother to the Nova Club crew, strode through the crowd and stopped beside the colonel, fixing him with a glare that had made more than one cyborg step back and rethink their life choices.

Archer shot her a look of irritation, "We're doing this here? Now?"

Phyl crossed her arms over her chest and nodded. "If you don't want to hear it, you could just agree to let her stay."

"You know I can't do that. Orders are—"

She slashed a hand through the air. "Don't you dare finish that sentence."

Colonel Scott Archer, commander of the Drift's armed forces base and legend in his own time, glared at Phyl and didn't say a word for several seconds.

Phyl lowered her voice. "Scott, you can't imprison them on that planet forever. Not if they want to leave. If you do that, then you're no better than the corporations that enslaved them in the first place."

Chance stepped up beside him, taking his hand. "I'm not a threat to anyone. Please. I want to stay here. If you send me back, I'll never be happy. I can't even go outside. The sky, the open spaces, I hate them."

"Agoraphobia?" Archer asked her, his tone gentler than it had been a moment before.

"Severe," she admitted.

He huffed out a frustrated breath.

"That information is not in your file."

"I was in cryo when that file was created. They couldn't note something no one knew."

"I understand you're not the spy we've been looking for, either."

She shook her head. "I'm not, but I'm certain I know who is. That's my skill set."

Archer nodded. "I know what you can do. And we'll find the spy. My people are working with Corp-Sec already."

She exhaled slowly and he felt her relax a little. "Phaedra was the one who told me about this place. I didn't realize it at the time, but I think, maybe, she was trying to tell me this was where I should be."

Archer pinched the bridge of his nose, a pained look crossing his features. "Kari. Of course she's involved in this."

Phyl chuckled. "You honestly thought she wasn't?"

Erik saw his opening and took it. "If Phaedra sent her here, then the Vardarians won't have any issues with her staying. I can't imagine the cyborgs will, either. Which means that the only one saying no right now is you, sir."

Archer sighed and looked at her intently. "If you stay here, you're going to need protection. You'd be safer back at the colony."

"I'll protect her," Erik stated.

"And so will we." Cynder declared as she joined the group.

"Yeah," Vic and Ward chimed in.

"You will?" Chance asked, hope suffusing her words.

"You're family, now. If we'd trusted you sooner, you might have helped us find the spy." Cynder smiled. "Sorry about that."

Chance cocked her head and gave Cyn a long look. "You had your reasons."

Cynder blinked, and then smiled a little. "Yeah. I did."

He'd missed something there, he was sure of it, but there were more pressing issues at the moment. "Anything else required, Sir?"

"Only a mountain of paperwork, and a long talk with an alien prince and some cyborg colonists." Archer narrowed his eyes at the two of them. "Which you will both be part of. This is not a done deal. Not even close. You understand that?"

"Yes, sir."

Archer nodded. "Good. Oh, and we'll have to discuss Chance's new duties, of course."

"Duties?" Chance asked.

"I'm seconding you. Welcome to the IAF."

Erik bristled. "No. You don't own her, Sir, and neither does the military." He respected Archer, but he didn't trust the organization he worked for. Not anymore.

"The only way to justify her staying here is to make her an asset," Archer said.

"But she's not an asset. Chance is a person, free to make her own choices." He turned to smile at her. "And for the record, sweet thing, I'm hoping I'm one of the choices you make."

"For the record? I already made that choice." She squeezed his hand and gave him a radiant smile.

Cynder spoke up. "What about hiring her as a consultant? You'd get the benefit of her skills without forced conscription. That might be best for everyone." Cynder glanced around at the soldiers standing between them and the restless crowd. "You're supposed to be protecting us, not taking over our lives."

Those close enough to hear her comment nodded in agreement, and word spread through the crowd, drawing more affirmative comments and a few angry ones about the increased military presence on the station.

"If I were a consultant, I'd be able to work with others, too. Maybe Corp-Sec? Nova Force? I'd like to help, but only if I can choose how. What I can do…" Chance shook her head. "I won't be used as a weapon."

A blaze of pride flashed through him as she stood her ground against Archer. She was too good for him, but that wasn't going to stop him from making her his, forever.

CHANCE HAD to keep her emotions under tight control or she was going to start crying. Cyborgs didn't cry. It was one of the unwritten rules.

She was still trying to grasp all that had happened. These beings might have come because Erik had asked for help, but they were staying for her. Cynder had named her family. It was a high compliment, and one she was determined to live up to. An hour ago she'd thought she had lost everything. Now, she had more than she had dared to hope for, including Erik. At least she would, if Colonel Archer said yes.

Phyl dropped her voice to a low murmur. "Don't repeat past mistakes, Scott. You know what's right. This time, you can make a different choice."

A flash of regret showed in Archer's eyes for a second. "You know I didn't have a choice last time."

"And you know I don't believe that. But that's the past. This is now." Phyl inclined her head toward Chance. "What's it going to be?"

Archer considered a moment, then nodded. "I think making her a consultant could work. I'll talk to the heads of the colony. Until then, someone needs to take responsibility for Chance." He looked at Erik. "I'm assuming you're willing, Lieutenant Commander?"

"Yes, sir. It would be my honor to do so. But I would like to request that you stop using my former rank. I resigned my commission years ago. And if you know my rank, then you know why I quit."

And when they were alone again, she wanted to hear that story. There was so much she didn't know about Erik. But now, they'd have time to learn about each other. Still, she knew the most important stuff already. He was kind and brave. He'd been there for her when she'd needed him, and she loved him. It was too soon to say anything, but that didn't change the facts. Nothing would.

There'd be time to talk about that, later. Time for questions, for answers, and to get to know her new family, including the ones whose blood she shared. But that was later, for now, all she needed was Erik.

"Very well." Archer glanced around them. "Now that things are decided, can I assume that this crowd will be dispersing?"

Erik shrugged. "They're here because they were worried about Chance. She's been through a lot today. If I take her out of here, I'm sure they'll move on."

"Then I suggest you do so." Archer managed to make the *suggestion* sound like an order.

Erik grinned. "Yes, sir. Happy to." He turned to her. "Arms around my neck, sweet thing. We're leaving."

"Yes, sir. Happy to." She repeated his words with a joyful laugh and threw her arms around his neck. He swept her into his arms and started walking. The soldiers gave way, then the crowd beyond them, everyone cheering as they saw what was happening.

"I still can't believe it. All these people…"

"Are here because they care about you."

"And you do, too?" She knew the answer already, but she wanted to hear him say it.

Erik stopped walking, then bowed his head to kiss her softly. "I care about you. Very much."

"Oh good," she purred and lifted her head to kiss him hungrily. "because there's a one hundred percent chance that I feel the same way."

"Is that so?" he asked when he finally raised his

head again and started walking. "In that case, what do you think the odds are that we're going to my room right now and not leaving until tomorrow?"

A rush of desire washed over her, leaving her flushed and suddenly hungry for more than kisses. "They better be a hundred percent, or I'm going to be very disappointed. I haven't even seen your quarters yet."

"I will do my best to never disappoint you. And I'm sorry I kept you away from my quarters. Cynder and the others didn't want you to have access to that area. They were protecting the sprites."

"I understand. Nothing is more important than family." She knew Cyn was protecting more than just her nieces, but that wasn't her news to share.

"But you're family now. You're *mine*, now."

"Your family?" The word resonated through her, filling the holes in her heart with a sense of warmth and hope she'd never known before.

Erik was smiling as he leaned down to kiss her again. "My everything."

CHANCE DIDN'T GET to see much of Erik's quarters the first time she saw them. He walked right through the main area and straight into the sanitation room.

"I thought we were going to bed?" she asked.

"Oh, that's on the agenda. But I figured you might like to shower first. I've found it's a good way to move past a bad day or a traumatic event."

She had to agree with him. The idea of scrubbing away the memories of being manhandled, threatened, and hurt was appealing right now. "That sounds good."

"I thought so. Plus, this gives me a chance to check you over and make sure those medics didn't miss anything." He set her down and started stripping out of his clothes.

"What are you going to do if you find anything?"

"Kiss it better, of course."

"That won't fix anything." Not that she was opposed to letting him kiss her anywhere he wanted to, but she didn't see the point.

"Right. You never had anyone to kiss your boo-boo's better. Well, trust me, it helps. Get in the shower, and I'll prove it to you."

She was more than happy to follow his suggestion. There wasn't much room for the two of them to undress in the small room, and she bumped into the cold metal walls more than once. There was even less room in the shower stall. "How are we both going to fit in there?"

Erik gathered up their clothes and tossed them into the main room. "We don't. Computer, reconfigure the sanitation room to Torski shower setting."

"The what?"

"Watch this." Erik pulled her in close as metallic shutters extended from the walls to cover the towel racks and toiletries. A cubby opened in the wall beside them, revealing several dispensers she assumed were full of cleanser. Another panel slid open above, and a showerhead dropped into place.

"Convertible space. Nice. And very sensible."

"It also means I've got a personal steam room, which is a real luxury after a fight night. Even with water restrictions, I can enjoy a nice steam any time I want."

"Will you understand if I don't go to your next fight? I just...I don't want to watch that. It's not that I don't think you're capable, it's that I had to watch them make some of the other cyborgs on the station fight each other. It...It was bad."

He kissed her bare shoulder. "I'm not going back into the ring, Chance. I hadn't admitted it to myself yet, but there's a reason I haven't been back in the cage in two months. I don't need it anymore."

"You needed it? Why?"

"I'll explain later. I promise."

The calculation took less than a second to make. "This is about your time in the IAF, isn't it?"

"It is. Computer, turn on the shower with water temperature three degrees lower than default setting."

The shower came on a few seconds later, and just as Erik had promised, the room quickly filled with billowing clouds of steam. It was heavenly, and so was the way his hands moved over her water-slick skin. His mouth crushed down on hers, and she stopped thinking about anything but him. Hot water poured over them, adding heat to the fire he was kindling with every kiss and caress.

They washed each other, arousal blending with ritual as they wiped away every reminder of the ordeal they'd gone through. Only once they were done did his touch grow hungrier, his kisses so demanding that all she could do was give herself over to the need coursing through her.

Her fingers found his cock and he groaned into her mouth, rocking his hips against her touch. "Want you."

"I'm all yours. "

"Then I'm the luckiest man in the galaxy." He backed her against the nearest wall and kissed her again, a soul-deep kiss that made her heart soar higher than the stars. He lifted her and she happily wrapped her arms around his neck, holding herself in place as he settled himself between her legs, never once breaking their kiss.

She twined her legs around his hips, moaning into his mouth when he worked a hand between them to toy with her clit. When he slid two fingers into her channel, she shivered and bucked her hips, craving deeper contact. "More."

"*Fraxx*, yes. I'll give you more." He withdrew his hand and replaced it with the thick head of his cock, pushing into her with one slow, steady thrust that pinned her against the wall, gasping softly.

That's the sound I love best in the galaxy," he murmured.

She laughed and nuzzled his cheek. "Mine is hearing you say my name as you come."

His cock jerked inside her, and he growled her name in warning. Instead of replying, she flexed her inner walls around him and tightened her legs around his hips. After that, it didn't take long for both of them to lose control.

They made love to each other in the warm cocoon of

his shower, skin sliding across skin, the two of them racing towards release, lost to everything but each other.

They came within seconds of each other, and she smiled as he called her name as his orgasm tore through him, his thrusts wild and erratic as he emptied himself inside her. It really was her favorite sound.

They stayed that way, tangled and breathless, until the thirty-second warning sounded, announcing they were about to run out of water for the day. They raced to rinse off before the shower ended, then wandered into the main room to towel off. He lured her into bed with a promise of snuggles. Until Erik, she'd never experienced that kind of post-sex intimacy, and she loved every second they spent that way.

Once she was nestled in his arms, her head on his chest and their legs intertwined, she uttered a contented sigh. "I like this."

"Me too. I've wanted to get you into my bed since the moment we met. Hell, if I'm being honest, that plan started before we officially met."

"It did?"

"Mhmm. I knew what I wanted the second I set eyes on you, sweet thing." His voice was a low, satisfied rumble beneath her ear.

"I wanted you, too. You were the first man I've ever fantasized about."

"Better be the only one, too."

"Tell me something about yourself, Erik. You know all my secrets, but I don't know yours."

"You know I'm afraid of snakes," he pointed out.

"Okay, I know one thing."

He kissed her brow. "You want to know about my time in the military." It wasn't a question.

"I want to know what happened to make you resign."

"I was an officer in the IAF, you know that already. Years ago, I was sent to a planet to deal with a conflict between a corporation and a group of settlers. At least, we learned later they were settlers. The corporation claimed they were raiding ships, trading in sex slaves and weapons. We went there to wipe them out, but all we found were farmers."

"What happened to them?"

Erik sighed and she felt him tense. "They died. I refused to follow orders, and my men stood with me, but others didn't. They followed their orders without question, and those poor people died. They didn't have ships to raid with. Hell, they barely had any weapons. They couldn't defend themselves, and I didn't defend them, either."

"But you didn't attack them." She couldn't imagine being ordered to attack innocents, but she knew her combat cyborg brethren had been forced to do that, and worse. In some ways, she was grateful she'd been kept in a lab.

"No, we didn't. But by the time my report made it through the ranks to someone not being influenced by the corporation who'd sent us here, it was too late. I should have done more."

"If you'd defended them, what would have happened?"

"We would have had to fight our own people. There would have been deaths on both sides. Wait, are you trying to analyze the situation so you can tell me there wasn't a good outcome to be had?"

"Maybe. Though I don't have much data to go on."

"I don't need you to run the numbers to tell me that that op was going to go to shit no matter what choice I made." He tapped his head, then his chest. "My brain knows that. It's my heart that still wonders if I should have tried anyway."

"You can't save everyone, love. Sometimes, it's all you can do to save yourself."

"For a long time, I thought what I did made me a coward. I tried to down myself in pharma and booze and punished myself by going into the ring again and again. This place, and the people in it, helped me work through all that. It's been a long road, but worth every step of the journey."

She raised her head to smile at him. "Because you have friends, family, and a new purpose now?"

"All of that, yeah." He rose up to kiss her, his hand tangling in her hair to draw her in close. "But mostly because at the end of the road, I found you."

CHAPTER NINE

ERIK HATED FEELING POWERLESS, especially when someone he cared about was at risk. They'd been preparing for this test of her abilities since the day she'd agreed to consult for the IAF, but he still wasn't ready. Nearly two weeks had passed since he'd almost lost her, and he felt like he was facing that whole nightmare of a day over again. "You're sure you're ready for this?"

Chance gave an almost imperceptible nod. She couldn't move her head more than that because every data port in her skull was being used to jack her into the IAF's computer system. Well, part of it, anyway. To protect Chance, and the system, from overload, she was accessing a single computer with no outside connections. Not that it made him feel better about any of this. There was still more data in that one computer than Chance had ever attempted to absorb before. If something went wrong…

He dropped into a crouch in front of her. "Hey,

sweet thing. Before you do this, there's something you need to know."

She gifted him with a sweet, knowing smile. "There's a very good chance I know what you're about to say."

"Well, you're going to hear it, anyway, my sexy little know-it-all." He took her hands in his and tried to ignore the fact that his family and friends were all gathered in the observation room above them and could hear every word he said. "I love you, Chance, and I'm planning on spending the rest of my life with you, so nothing can go wrong today. You hear me?"

She grinned. "Are you trying to give me orders again?"

"This is one order I need you to follow, sweet thing."

She squeezed his hands. "I've done the calculations a dozen times. It's going to be fine."

"You don't know that."

"Yes, I do. Because I have plans, too. I love you, and I want to wake up beside you every day I'm breathing, so I'm going to be fine because anything else isn't in my plans."

A chorus of cheers came from the observation room, but he didn't turn to look. He kept his focus on Chance. "Sound's like they're happy for us."

"At least now we can finally find out who won the betting pool. I think they owe us a drink."

"Absolutely. We could blow this gig and collect right now if you like?" He was teasing her – mostly.

"I need to do this, Erik. It's what I was made for."

"I know. We all need a purpose." He knew that

better than some. The club and the friends he had there had become his purpose in life, bringing him back from the edge when he'd had nothing left to live for. They'd talked about this, and he'd already agreed that it was something she needed to do. He just didn't want Archer or anyone else pushing her to do too much before she was ready. Chance felt like she needed to prove herself, but that wasn't true at all. Cynder and everyone at the Nova Club were doing all they could to make up for their earlier distrust. She had full access to the club's residential areas now, and she had fallen in love with the sprites once she'd been allowed to meet the club's youngest members.

It helped that Kirk had been caught and confessed to everything. The asshole had been busy in his short time at the club - skimming money from the tables, selling unlicensed pharma, and of course, spying on everyone who worked there.

Erik would have loved to get his hands on Kirk himself for a bit of payback, but he'd had to settle for letting Cyn, Kit, and Luke handle that. Kirk had tried to stow away on a cargo freighter, and the captain was a friend of Phylomenia's. He'd brought the sniveling weasel back to Astek and punted him off the ship a few minutes early, giving Cynder, her husbands, and her two brothers time to teach the spying bastard a harsh lesson about the price of betrayal. Kirk had risked the lives of everyone that mattered to Erik, all in the name of greed. Whatever cell he was rotting in, Erik hoped he was there for a long *fraxxing* time.

Lieksa cleared her throat. "We're ready."

Erik gave Chance's fingers one last squeeze. "Good luck." Then, he rose to his feet to take his place on the far side of the room.

The observation room was above and behind him, full of beings who were here to support Chance. Archer had grumbled about getting everyone clearance for what was supposed to be a secret test, but he'd given in eventually. Chance had made it easier for him by selecting a calculation that wouldn't reveal mission sensitive information.

Erik knew why she'd picked that subject, but not many others did. Not yet. He was almost sorry he'd miss seeing their faces when she announced her calculations, but he wasn't leaving this room until Chance did.

The only people he knew inside this room were Lieksa and Eric Erben. Lieksa was a cybernetic tech and a good friend. Eric was a cyber-jockey with Nova Force, and the closest thing they had to an onsite expert in human-computer interfacing. The three of them were the only ones in the room who were more interested in Chance's wellbeing than her abilities and what they meant for the IAF.

"Proceed when ready," Archer's voice came over the room's speakers. He was in the observation area with the others.

Erik wanted to pace, but he couldn't. He just kept his gaze locked on Chance and waited.

It didn't take long. She sat up, laid her hands in her lap, and winked at him.

"Ready."

"Activating datalink," one of the techs announced.

Chance's eyes closed and her body went rigid. She was so still he swore she wasn't even breathing. For that matter, neither was he.

Another tech kept announcing the time every thirty seconds. One minute. Two. Three. Chance had warned him that it would take five or more minutes for her to parse the volume of data she'd chosen for today's test, but that didn't stop him from worrying as the time crawled by and she didn't so much as flutter an eyelash.

At the four-minute mark, he started fantasizing about punching the tech reading out the time. By seven minutes, he was ready to demand they shut it all down. Before the tech could call out another interval, she finally opened her eyes.

"Calculation complete," she announced in a weak, shaky voice.

He almost flew across the room to her, arriving before anyone else could. "You okay?"

"I'm okay. Juice, please?"

She'd told him these sessions always left her with a dry mouth and a nasty headache that not even her medi-bots could fix quickly. He handed her the squeeze-tab of orange juice he'd brought for her and she took a few sips. "How's the head?"

"Ow. Worst headache yet, but that's not surprising. I've never tried to extrapolate that much data before."

"You need a painblocker?" he asked.

"I could block it myself, but the meds will work longer."

Lieksa appeared beside them, already holding an injector in her hand. "How bad is the pain?"

"Like I've got a Nantari rhino tapdancing inside my head in stiletto heels."

Lieksa made a quick adjustment to the dosage and pressed the injector to Chance's arm.

"Let me know if you need another dose. Any other issues?"

Chance beamed. "None. It worked perfectly."

"Yeah?" he asked, sensing her excitement. "Were you right?"

"I was. Can we get me unplugged? I really want to tell everyone before the fatigue kicks in and all I want to do is sleep."

Lieksa and several other techs set about disconnecting her from the system as carefully as if she'd been made of glass. Which is exactly what he'd told them to do. The first time they'd practiced this, one of the techs had been careless, pulling Chance's hair and complaining that his job would be easier if they shaved her head. Erik had restrained himself, and the tech had only lost his job… and a couple of teeth.

Chance had warned them about the fatigue, too. The bigger the calculation, the more time it took for her to recover. Her nanotech could manage almost any physical issue, but these sorts of calculations were mentally exhausting. It would take a week or more for her to recover enough to be able to do this again. He suspected it was one of the reasons she'd been placed in cryo on Reamus Station before they'd even finished testing her abilities. The Gray Men wanted results, and they wanted them quickly. She would never be able to give them that. As far as they were concerned, she was a failed experiment, and he was grateful they hadn't seen her value. If they had, he'd still have a hole in his life and his heart that only Chance could fill.

"All clear. How are you feeling?" Lieksa asked.

"Painblocker is working, and so is the juice. I'm as good as I'm going to get for now." Chance looked at him with a tired smile. "Help me up?"

He held out his hands and drew her up to her feet. He wanted to scoop her into his arms and carry her all the way back to their quarters, but he couldn't do that to her. She'd accomplished what she'd set out to do and she deserved to stay and enjoy this moment.

She leaned in and stole a quick kiss. "I promise you can whisk me away from all this soon, Shoulders. In fact, I'm looking forward to curling up in bed with you and telling you everything I discovered, but for now, I want to share the highlights with our friends."

"You mean our family."

Her smile could have lit up half a solar system. "Yes, I do."

Stars above and below, he loved this woman, and it did his heart good to see her so happy. "Better tell them, then."

CHANCE'S HEAD hurt and she felt like she could sleep for a week, but nothing was going to stop her from enjoying this moment. Erik moved in beside her, lending her silent support by wrapping a strong arm around her waist and drawing her in close to his side. Above them, everyone was watching. She could only see a few faces clearly, but she knew they were all there.

"Colonel Archer, you'll be happy to hear that the test was a complete success. I managed to absorb and parse all the data and make some calculations. We'll need to verify my findings to confirm their accuracy, but I'm confident everything worked."

"How soon…" Archer started to ask a question and was interrupted by Phyl discreetly elbowing him in the midsection. He shot Phyl a look of mild annoyance with a faint hint of amusement, cleared his throat, and started again. "What I meant to ask is, how are you feeling, Chance?"

"The pain is being managed by painblockers and I'm going to need to rest, but I'm not experiencing anything beyond what we expected."

Archer nodded, his expression showing a moment of honest relief. "Glad to hear it."

He waited a beat before adding. "Do you have something you'd like to share with us?"

Archer was one of only three people she'd told about her conviction she was genetically linked to some of the cyborgs present. It's why she'd chosen to this particular chunk of data to test her abilities. It wasn't a full-on prediction of future events, but that would come soon.

"Yes, sir. I do. With your permission?"

"Go ahead." This time he actually smiled at her as he granted her permission to share what she'd learned.

"Time to blow their minds, sweet thing," Erik whispered in her ear.

"For today's test, Colonel Archer arranged for me to have access to the complete list of names and genetic data from the Vault of the Fallen, a genetic repository for the IAF's greatest fallen heroes." There was a murmur of surprise from the speaker, and she could see everyone crowding closer to the glass so they could see her.

"Though it's generally a secret few outside this room are aware of, you all know that some of that DNA was stolen by the Gray Men and used to create cyborgs. Us. Today, I took that data and compared it to the genetic makeup of every cyborg here, including myself. And before you worry about who has that information, I had help from Lieksa with that part."

Lieksa laughed and waved at the group above. "Surprise."

"Keeping secrets from us, Angel? That's going to cost you!" one of Lieksa's husbands called out. Chance couldn't tell if it was Mack or Dash.

"You might want to hold off on her punishment until you hear what I learned. I know who our ancestors were. And…" She took a deep breath. "I know that I'm related to some of you. Not a batch-sibling, but almost that close. Batch-cousins, I suppose."

"Who?" Someone demanded.

"Toro, Jaeger, Vic, and Ward."

Cynder laughed long and hard. "I've got another sister-in-law!"

She waited for the four men to say something, but

none of them said a word. She was worried they weren't happy until Toro barrelled through the door, followed by his batch-brothers. The next thing she knew, she was caught up in a rib-creaking hug. "Holy *fraxx*, welcome to the family!"

"Easy, Toro. That's my girl you're crushing there. I'd like her back in one piece, big guy."

Ward took her from Toro and hugged her. "I'm sorry about before. What we thought you'd done…"

"You thought you were protecting the people you care about. You don't need to apologize for that."

"But you're family!" Ward's voice cracked a little on the last word.

"And you protected me when I needed it most." Eventually, she'd tell them when she realized their connection, but it wouldn't be today.

"*Veth*. Hold up. Erik is dating our little sister. As her older brothers, how do we feel about this?" Vic asked.

"I'm not technically your sister. Different batches," she reminded them as she finally freed herself from another hug.

"Nope. You're our sister. End of conversation," Toro declared.

"Which means you're going to be an aunt," Cynder announced as she joined the others.

"Yeah!" Jaeger pulled Cynder in for a kiss. "Still can't believe that."

"Wait, what?" Everyone upstairs started asking questions, and soon they were all crowded into the testing room instead of waiting upstairs. There was plenty of laughter, hugs, and congratulations for all, and she got to tell each of them a little about who their ancestors were, with a promise to give them a full write up once she'd had time to rest.

The room buzzed as the names Sato, Allen, Hill, Jelani, Kallson, and others were spoken aloud for the first time.

She and Erik managed to find Cynder in the crowd. "Now that I can finally say it, I wanted to offer my congratulations."

Erik nodded. "When Chance told me, I understood why you did what you did when you found out about the spy. You weren't just protecting the sprites." His gaze dropped to Cyn's still-flat stomach. "You were protecting your own child, too."

"I was. I was wrong, though. Chance was never a threat. She's family." The big cyborg woman folded them both into a fierce hug and dropped her voice to a whisper. "And thank you, I'm so in love with this baby already and it's not even born yet."

"I don't know much about offspring or combat, but whatever you need from me, I'll do my best to protect you and your little one," Chance promised.

"Same here. No one messes with our family," Erik agreed.

Cyn grinned. "Damn right they don't."

After that, they made their escape, leaving the rest to talk about the day's successes and surprises. She managed to make it to the club before exhaustion hit, and she didn't protest when Erik swept her into his arms and carried her the rest of the way home.

She never got tired of that word. The Nova was her

home now. The first one she'd ever had. The Haven colony had been exactly that, a haven where she had learned what freedom meant, but it had never been her home.

"You still with me, sweet thing?" Erik asked as they passed through the door into his room."

"Always." She didn't need to calculate the odds that they'd be together forever to know it was true. She'd found her place in the galaxy, and the other half of her heart. She wasn't going anywhere, now, or ever. If the odds said differently, then she'd find a way to change them. She was his everything, and he was hers.

***

Thank You for Reading Chance Of A Lifetime!

I hope you enjoyed Erik and Chance's story
If you're looking for more stories like this one, I invite
you to explore the other books in the <u>Drift</u> universe,
which include both the <u>Nova Force</u> and <u>Drift</u> series.